OTTO PENZLER PRESENTS
AMERICAN MYSTERY CLASSICS

THE ALARM OF
THE BLACK CAT

DOLORES HITCHENS (1907–1973) was a highly prolific mystery author who wrote under multiple pseudonyms and in a range of styles. A large number of her books, including *The Alarm of the Black Cat*, were published under the D. B. Olsen moniker, but she is perhaps best remembered today for her later novel, *Fool's Gold*, published under her own name, which was adapted for film as *Band a part* by Jean-Luc Godard.

DAVID HANDLER is the Edgar Award-winning, critically acclaimed author of several bestselling mystery series. He began his career as a New York City reporter, and wrote his first two novels—*Kiddo* (1987) and *Boss* (1988)—about his Los Angeles childhood. In 1988 he published *The Man Who Died Laughing*, the first of his long-running series of mysteries starring ghostwriter Stewart Hoag and his faithful basset hound Lulu.

THE ALARM OF
THE BLACK CAT

DOLORES
HITCHENS

Writing as
D.B. Olsen

Introduction by
DAVID
HANDLER

AMERICAN
MYSTERY
CLASSICS

Penzler Publishers
New York

Published in 2023 by Penzler Publishers
58 Warren Street, New York, NY 10007
penzlerpublishers.com

Distributed by W. W. Norton

Cover image: Andy Ross
Cover design: Mauricio Diaz

Paperback ISBN 978-1-61316-392-4
Hardcover ISBN 978-1-61316-393-1

Library of Congress Control Number: 2022917458

Printed in the United States of America

9 8 7 6 5 4 3 2 1

INTRODUCTION

DOLORES HITCHENS is not a familiar name to crime fiction fans these days, even though she was an incredibly prolific and versatile mid-twentieth century Southern California author of suspense, private detective novels and intricate murder mysteries that she wrote under her own name as well as several pseudonyms, most notably D.B. Olsen. The woman was no slouch. Her 1958 suspense novel *Fools' Gold* was turned into a film by Jean-Luc Godard, who was no slouch himself.

Yet when I mentioned her name to friends who are ardent mystery readers I draw nothing but blank stares, which is a real shame. Dolores Hitchens was not only a superior storyteller but a gifted wordsmith. Try this image on for size: "She shuddered all over; the act reminded Miss Rachel of a policeman's stallion she had once seen, forced to submit to being tied to a dead dray horse and to pull it off the street. There was the same ripple under the flesh, looseness of bone, look of uncomprehending horror."

Downright jaw dropping, am I right?

Among Hitchens' many accomplishments was her series of twelve intricate, tightly crafted, Rachel Murdock mysteries. *The Alarm of the Black Cat*, which was published in 1942, is the second volume in the series. Miss Rachel—and she's always referred to as Miss Rachel—is a trim, fragile little seventy-year-old spinster with snow-white hair and a modest manner who dresses in taffeta skirts and smells of lavender. Her dearest companion is a marmalade cat named Samantha. One of the characters in *The Alarm of the Black Cat* refers to Miss Rachel as "mildly eccentric" and "the sweet-old-lady type."

As I was stretched out on my sofa on a cold, rainy day savoring this genuine treat of a novel—my own nineteen-pound tabby, Leon, dozing on my chest—I was struck by how the passage of eight decades has changed our view of older women. I have several women friends who are over seventy and, trust me when I tell you that they are anything but fragile, modest little creatures. They run, bike, practice yoga, hold down full-time jobs and possess vastly more energy and robust good health than their sagging male counterparts.

Despite Miss Rachel's portrayal as frail and elderly, she has plenty to offer when it comes to smarts. She is a keen, intuitive observer who possesses such a cunning, cynical mind that it borders on hard-boiled. This is not to suggest she is Sam Spade in taffeta, but she does possess a very dark view of human nature and the evil, greedy behavior that we are capable of. Miss Rachel is also utterly fearless. Doesn't hesitate for one second to descend a rickety basement stairway in total darkness because she thinks she's heard an unusual noise down there. That unusual noise, it should come as no surprise, has something to do with a murder.

So, when it comes to Miss Rachel and her sidekick, Samantha, the somewhat plodding Lieutenant Mayhew has come to learn that attention must be paid.

The Alarm of the Black Cat takes place on Beecher Street, a short residential block that consists of four rather creepy old houses. Think Charles Addams. I did. Miss Rachel has recently rented one, giving her a bird's eye view of the other three houses, which seem to share a garden courtyard, possibly because the three families that own them have intertwining family connections that span four generations.

Lacking for drama Beecher Street is not. Among the plot ingredients Miss Rachel encounters, practically before she's unpacked her bags, are an unloved little girl's crushed toad, a deceased young wife whose husband was having an affair with their next door neighbor, a purloined letter, a dying lady with a hotly contested will, a valuable trust fund, someone who is spying on everyone from an upstairs window by candle light, a lot of creepy footsteps in Miss Rachel's very own house in the middle of the night, a dead body stuffed in a closet in her very own cellar, an unloved little girl's crushed toad (I know, I know, I already mentioned the crushed toad but I just had to do it again) and more suspects with more motives than you can possibly imagine.

Or, as Miss Rachel puts it, "There must be a great deal going on in these three houses, a great deal of worry and hatred and intrigue, of old scores being settled and new plottings being hatched."

Sound intriguing? Trust me, it is.

I was particularly pleased that Samantha the cat turns out to be no mere lap companion. She is of great service to Miss Rachel, especially in the climax of this fine novel. I happen to be a big, big fan of mysteries that feature pet sidekicks. In fact, I'm such a huge fan that out of the twenty-eight crime novels that I've published so far in my career fully two dozen of them—my thirteen Stewart Hoag mysteries and eleven Berger-Mitrys—feature four-legged characters in pivotal roles.

It's particularly true of my star novelist, Stewart Hoag, who crashed and burned and is now forced to eke out an ignoble living as a lowly ghostwriter of celebrity memoirs. Hoagy would be totally lost without his faithful, neurotic, breath-challenged basset hound, Lulu, who stays by his side morning, noon and night to make sure he stays in one piece. Hoagy doesn't just keep Lulu around for her comely good looks. Bassets are the second highest rated scent hounds in the dog world—only bloodhounds rank higher. She also possesses, like Miss Rachel's Samantha, a form of animal intuition that we humans do not. Face it, if a cat or dog takes an instant dislike to someone you can be damned sure that there's a good reason.

Again, attention must be paid.

But so must a price. Sadly, in today's mystery fiction world, the fact that Miss Rachel's Samantha plays a critical role in *The Alarm of the Black Cat* means that Very Serious experts are likely to dismiss it as a tea cozy, a poisonous label that I've gotten stuck with myself from time to time because of Hoagy's sidekick, Lulu. So don't get me started on the subject. Too late, you got me started. Just, please, do me a huge favor and think of *The Alarm of the Black Cat* as a traditional mystery, *not* a tea cozy. The label tea cozy immediately relegates a novel to second-class status as a cutesy diversion that is lacking in depth or seriousness of literary purpose. Take it from one who knows—nothing could be further from the truth.

All of which is to say I thoroughly enjoyed this book and fully intend to savor the rest of the Rachel Murdock series whenever I'm looking to be humbled by a storyteller vastly superior to what I can ever hope to be. These novels totally rock.

Just don't call them tea cozies. I mean it.

DAVID HANDLER
Old Lyme, Connecticut

THE ALARM OF
THE BLACK CAT

CHAPTER ONE

THERE ARE times when Miss Rachel Murdock considers that the solution of murders should be left to the general public.

More specifically, she remembers the case which she has pleased to call the Affair of the Little Meannesses. By Little Meannesses she refers to a number of things which to the official mind might have meant nothing: the burying of glass in the path of an old woman's fingers, the shutting in of a cat, the spoiling of a swing, and the death of a toad.

It was the toad, in the role of innocent bystander, who first savored the particularly brutal kind of death which hovered over the four houses at the end of Beecher and Chatham streets. The toad, drowsy in the heat of the underside of a rosebush, looked up to meet the face of Murder, and he died as befits a gentleman, quietly and without too much struggle. Perhaps he knew at that moment, by some divine dispensation, that his dying lessened and relieved, though only temporarily, the stored hatred which was soon to infect the neighborhood. But this is fancy; the heel which had mangled the toad, after wiping itself on the turf, walked away with a new caution, so that perhaps the murder of the toad had best be chalked up to practice.

The toad was eventually found by the little girl who had been in the habit of feeding him flies; he was wept over, wrapped in tissue paper, and put into a shoe box for decent burial. But between prayer and covering, between the last look of love and the first odor of dissolution, Miss Rachel saw him, and so he had not died in vain.

Whether Miss Rachel had any business being at the end of Beecher Street is a matter for debate, but the necessity for her seeing the toad is above question.

Miss Rachel will say that she happened to be at the end of Beecher Street because she needed to rent a house. This is a rank untruth; Miss Rachel owns a house in which she has lived these many years with her sister Jennifer. The fact is that at the age of seventy Miss Rachel has become restless with a desire for travel. She has discovered that one of the cheapest and most comfortable modes of travel in and about Los Angeles and Hollywood is by means of a rental agent's automobile. The question of the cost of gasoline and oil has never worried her. To Jennifer's fret about the ethics of letting rental agents cart her about to numberless houses which she had no intention of renting, Miss Rachel makes the simple reply that she did actually rent a house.

For a month, Miss Jennifer sniffs.

This remark always rouses in Miss Rachel a mild wonder that so few days could contain so much mystery and creeping, relentless horror. That the little toad, dead in his cardboard coffin, could have been the forerunner of days of blood, nights of fear, and hours when Miss Rachel peeped from under her blinds with a core of terror inside her drawn tight as a fiddlestring. That the month of September, slipping off the calendar, marked the end of an eternity of watchfulness, a lifetime of breath-stopping dread.

She sometimes wonders what the net result might have been if she had never seen Mr. Toad at all.

The rental agent was a round, smooth little man dressed in a bright blue suit and possessed with a determination to please. His car was a sedan, almost new, and he drove it well; so well that Miss Rachel allowed him a second day of her time. It was on this second day that he took her to the vacant house at the end of Beecher Street.

Beecher Street begins with the dwindlings of an outlying shopping district in Los Angeles; it climbs hill of flats and scattered shops; it descends into a valley of old mansions and a park; it keeps bravely paved onward through an empty subdivision, and it ends on a grassy flat beyond which rise the blue Santa Monica foothills. It was in the shadow of these foothills, late in the afternoon, that Miss Rachel stepped from the rental agent's car to inspect a house.

It was a gray house built in the style of 1910, two-storied, with a big front porch, bulging windows, much latticework and trimmings. The garden was gone to weeds. The gate squeaked. On either side were two other houses, one white and one brown, with gardens well kept and with a look of having been long lived in.

Miss Rachel smoothed her taffeta skirt away from the reach of a nail in the gatepost, went up the path with the agent following, and stood on the porch while he inspected his keys.

The front door opened upon gloom and an odor of old wallpaper.

The agent said, "This isn't at all new, of course, but it's very reasonable. Thirty-five a month. Might be had for thirty, providing you'd sign a lease for it." He tried to pierce the placid expression of Miss Rachel's face for any interest she might feel. "Would you perhaps like to see the rooms?"

Miss Rachel, having in mind a good view of the hills with the sun going down behind them, suggested starting with the upstairs, rear. The puzzled little man preceded her, opened doors, and made a rambling sales talk. He by now considered Miss Rachel mildly eccentric, though she was still classified in his mind as the sweet-old-lady type, and he liked the way she smelled of lavender.

Miss Rachel looked for the hills through a sparkling pane. What she discovered was the little girl burying her toad.

"It's a very private neighborhood," the agent pointed out. "You'll notice there are just these four houses on the entire block. No traffic. The street ends just below."

"Mmmmmm," said Miss Rachel.

The little girl was saying a prayer over the open grave. She had her eyes shut tight and her grubby hands pressed up under her chin.

It occurred to Miss Rachel that this particular window was exceptionally clean, considering the state of the rest of the house. She drew back a little. Faint in the dust that covered the floor were a man's footprints. Round blobs of wax, perhaps a dozen, decorated the sill and the floor. A circular imprint marked the center of the sill. But most odd of all was a scattering of cake crumbs which Miss Rachel, testing surreptitiously between her fingers, found fresh and moist.

Through the window she had an excellent view of the two back yards on either side and of the house across the weed-grown alley whose rear door faced her.

On the back porch stood a woman, heavy of body, whose

face shone out of the dusk and seemed to contemplate the little girl. In its Slavic simplicity Miss Rachel could read no expression whatever, but there was an air of watchfulness in the way she held her head. The little girl had begun to slide the box down into the hole she had made for it. Miss Rachel was possessed with a sudden desire to know what it was she was burying in the yard below.

The agent was busy pointing out the excellent condition of the doorknob, since he had heard that most elderly women lock themselves into their rooms at night. Miss Rachel brushed past.

"There are four bedrooms up here," he said quickly, going after. "The right front is the biggest, very lovely; the paper's in fine condition, and the . . . ah . . ."

Miss Rachel was tripping downstairs.

He followed with a sigh, resigning himself to not renting the house and wondering what his wife might be having for dinner. To his surprise Miss Rachel did not make for the front door. At the foot of the stairs she turned right toward the kitchen. He stared after her and heard the snap of the back-door latch and the squeak of a hinge as she went out.

In the weedy garden Miss Rachel walked with caution, fearing to alarm the child; when the little girl looked up Miss Rachel smiled.

The little girl did not smile back; the blue eyes were grave and the round chin very much under control.

"You have a pretty box," Miss Rachel said tactfully. "It seems a shame to put it in the ground."

The little girl put down a hand and smoothed the box lid gently. "My toadie's inside. I'm burying him because he's dead."

Miss Rachel's zeal went out with a quick flow. Whatever she had expected from the array of footprints in the empty house, the watching woman, the little girl with her box, it had not been the mere burial of a toad.

"This was his garden," the child went on quietly, "and he took care of the rosebushes when nobody else wanted them. Sometimes he let me feed him a little—flies, you know—and he wasn't afraid any more if I came up careful." She lifted the lid of the box, peeked in at the tissue paper, her face averted lest Miss Rachel catch a glimpse of tears. "I loved him, and now he's all mashed."

The juxtaposition of love and destruction caught Miss Rachel's thought, and she bent over. The child glanced at her quickly, as if to see whether the delicate little old lady were making fun. Some idea of Miss Rachel's sympathy reached her; she took the lid off the box and unfolded the tissue paper.

No look of revulsion marred Miss Rachel's countenance. She inspected the broken toad and saw that the creature's head was marked at one spot with what might have been the corner of a heel. The green skin gave evidences of trampling: soil and twigs and bits of leaf mold. The watery eyes looked serenely at nothing.

"I think he's gone to heaven now, don't you?" The little girl took anxious care with the fitting of the box lid. "He was nice; he was always here waiting when I wanted to play. He didn't bite or scratch, either."

"I think he's gone there," Miss Rachel agreed. She watched while the little girl covered the box and patted the earth to firmness. She judged the child to be about eight. Her clothes and hair and skin spoke of care and good taste. Her pink print dress was hemmed now with dust, but it must have been immaculate before the burial of the toad.

The child sat frowning for a moment; her light brows made a tangle where they met like a little mingling of feathers. "You know, I'd better mark this, hadn't I? I wouldn't want to forget. When the roses come again it would be nice to put a bouquet here." She inspected Miss Rachel as if for signs of disagreement.

"That's a sensible idea," Miss Rachel said. "Why not find a nice smooth stone and mark his name on it?"

The little girl looked about, stood up uncertainly. "I'll help you look for one," Miss Rachel went on.

"Oh. Would you?"

Miss Rachel began to search the ground and if she saw the puzzled face of the rental agent looking at her through the glass panel of the rear door, she gave no sign. Under a rosebush she found what she had sought, Mr. Toad's field of honor. She bent over and raked at the leaf mold with a thin, delicate hand and found heavy heel marks which had overlapped each other in the making. The heel was that of a man's shoe or of a woman's stout oxford. Remembering the condition of the toad, Miss Rachel had a sudden vision of fury and a chill.

She raised her head. The sky above was the clear luminous blue of after-sunset, the Santa Monica mountains a brown line to the north with a row of trees like a cockatoo's crest going up to the summit. In the high clear air a flock of swallows shone with reflected gold.

But the earth was darkening with a foretaste of night. Under the rosebushes lay the shadowy beginnings of twilight, and a stone which the little girl had found showed bone-white against the dusky earth.

To left and right the neighboring yards were empty, but across the alley the woman still watched them; watched, from what Miss Rachel could make out through the fringe of towering weeds, with a new and angry intensity. Her face floated there in the shadow of the entry, and its gaze never left the little girl.

A tremble of nervousness came over Miss Rachel. She wondered suddenly why she had happened to come here and what the rental agent really thought of her and what in heaven's name that foreign-looking woman found of so much interest in this deserted yard.

"Do you live there?" Miss Rachel asked, pointing, and thinking that perhaps the woman meant to watch over the child.

She looked up from placing the stone. "Across there?" She shook her head. "No, I live next door." She gestured toward the house to the right. "I live with Daddy and Aunt Bernice and Grandpa. It's Grandpa's house."

"Who's the—the lady?" Miss Rachel managed.

"Oh, that's Jessie." This was said without interest or resentment.

"Jessie?"

"She keeps house for Alma and Alma's mama."

"She's the maid there?"

The little girl nodded.

"Do you know that she's watching us?"

The child's glance flickered toward the weeds. "My daddy says she's a queer old duck. She watches, but she won't speak because my daddy almost married Alma once, only he married my mama instead."

"What does your mama think of her?" Miss Rachel asked shamelessly.

"Oh, my mama doesn't know. Mama died when I was little. I don't even remember about her, except I've seen her picture and she looked like a little girl. She had curls. Better than mine."

"What's your name?"

The child inspected her dirty hands. "My name's Claudia, and my last name's Byers, What's yours?"

"Miss Murdock."

"There's a man looking at you out of the back door."

"Yes, I know. I guess I'd better go. Perhaps I'll see you again sometime."

"Maybe you'll rent the house," Claudia offered.

Miss Rachel's thoughts skittered across thin ice. "Perhaps. I'm tempted to."

"If you do you mustn't be afraid."

"Afraid?"

"There's somebody walks around inside. I've heard them, and I've told Daddy, and he took away my book about the goblins, but I know it was real. The walking, I mean." She searched Miss Rachel for indications of disbelief.

"Well, that's interesting," Miss Rachel said. "Once when I heard it I climbed the meter box and looked into a window, but there wasn't anything. It must have been upstairs. I tore my dress on the meter box and had to stay in my own yard all the rest of the week, and I had to promise Grandpa I'd never climb up there again."

"And didn't you?"

The yellow head shook in negation. "I'd promised Grandpa and I couldn't."

"And you've never seen who it was who walked around?"

More headshaking. The dark blue eyes widened, grew eager.

"If you *do* come to live here could I come inside? Could I see upstairs?"

"We'll see when the time comes."

"That man's coming outside."

Miss Rachel turned to meet the advancing rental agent. She noted his expression of disillusionment.

He cast a lackluster eye over the garden. "This might be fixed up," he said mechanically. "The shrubs and roses are alive. If the weeds were cleared away and the walks rebricked it wouldn't be too bad."

"Who owns the property?" Miss Rachel asked.

The little man looked vague. "It's part of an estate held in trust. We pay the rent, less commission, to the bank which acts as executor. I'm not acquainted with the actual owner."

"Would I have to pay for the work done in the garden?"

He digested this slowly. "It would depend upon the kind of lease you would be willing to sign. On a long-term contract I believe the bank would allow for the garden repairs."

"Otherwise I should have to do them myself?"

He was beginning to be confused. "Do you mean you are interested in this property?"

Miss Rachel smoothed her taffeta skirt with a noncommittal hand. "I might be."

He was obviously trying to reorient himself to the idea of getting a fee from all this. His puzzled face surveyed Miss Rachel, the little girl, the garden gone blue with twilight. "I see. The rent, as I mentioned, is thirty-five per month. Short term, of course."

"I believe I'll try it for a month," Miss Rachel said quietly.

The rental agent's mouth opened, but no words came out of

it. Claudia touched the stiff taffeta of Miss Rachel's dress with shy interest. "Maybe you'll find out who it is," she whispered.

Miss Rachel had a quick image of herself peeping through the crack of a door to surprise an abashed and guilty prowler who promptly turned tail and ran.

She had no way of knowing, naturally, just how unexpected and how dreadful that encounter was to be.

CHAPTER TWO

MISS JENNIFER Murdock took the news of the house renting very poorly indeed; she lectured Miss Rachel on the fate that waits for fools and adventuresses.

It was early next morning. Miss Rachel stopped packing her suitcase long enough to glance at herself in the mirror. The word adventuress had struck her fancy. She inspected her looks with a new interest. What she saw was a trim little old lady with snow-white hair and a modest yet friendly eye. What she imagined is nobody's business.

"And you will not take the cat. Not this time, Rachel. You've dragged Samantha along with you before, and look what happened. Murders. Horrible murders."[1]

"I'll be very lonely," Miss Rachel pointed out, going back to her packing. "You can hire a housekeeper."

"No housekeeper's going to stay there and let me leave the doors open so that a prowler can come in and I can catch him."

Miss Jennifer pursed her spare mouth. "You shouldn't *want* to catch him. It's unnatural."

"Samantha could warn me. She mews at strangers sometimes."

---

1   *The Cat Saw Murder*, American Mystery Classics, 2021.

"The wrong times. You couldn't depend on her," Jennifer snapped.

The upshot of it was that Miss Rachel, packed and break-fasted, went off to buy a few sticks of secondhand furniture and Miss Jennifer set about finding Samantha's basket.

Miss Rachel bought a rug, three rocking chairs, an ancient radio, and an assortment of little tables. The little tables were added with the thought of how easily they could be tripped over in the dark by an unwary prowler. For the bedroom she purchased bed, springs, mattress, a rickety dressing table, and fireplace tongs. The tongs were a weapon, just in case.

Home again to collect her suitcase and a box of kitchen miscellany and Samantha, Miss Rachel admitted that she actually didn't know what to expect from her new adventure. "Perhaps it's just that they're all watching each other, for gossip or some other reason, and someone's started using the upstairs window in the empty house because it has a better view. I might never see the person. I might even find out that they're all friends."

"What about the toad?" Miss Jennifer asked.

A frown worried Miss Rachel's usually placid brow. "The toad is why I rented the place, of course. Just watching, spying, such as the foreign-looking woman was doing, could mean anything. Killing the toad and leaving him for Claudia to find was deliberate meanness. Somebody wanted to hurt the child. They did. They might want to hurt her again."

"You could go to her father about it," Miss Jennifer pointed out.

"Her father hasn't any imagination whatever, He wouldn't see it."

Miss Jennifer's stone-gray eyes widened in surprise, "But you don't even know Claudia's father!"

"I know that when Claudia told him she'd heard footsteps in the vacant house he took away her book about the goblins. If that isn't lack of imagination I'd like to know what is."

"Sounds like a sensible man to me," Miss Jennifer said and added irrelevantly, "and, besides, the toad might have got in the way."

"A toad under a rosebush isn't in anyone's way."

Miss Jennifer looked uncomfortable. In the light of the front-hall windows she seemed spare and forbidding; she had always lacked Rachel's demure appeal and had always been a little bit cross about it, and cross, too, because Rachel hadn't had the grace to be foolish as well as attractive. "If you get into trouble, Rachel, I must say that it will be just what you deserve."

Miss Rachel stooped and picked up Samantha's basket and kissed Jennifer on an unpowdered cheek. "I'll call on you, dear, if I need you."

Miss Jennifer shut her eyes as though this incorrigibility of Miss Rachel's were almost past endurance.

Miss Rachel went out softly toward the taxi and her great adventure.

That first day was taken up with the details of getting settled in the house at the end of Beecher Street.

Miss Rachel arranged the rug, the three rocking chairs, and the ancient radio in the living room, where they were dismally inadequate as far as filling the floor space went. One little table she put in the hall near the front door; one she put near the kitchen entrance. Two more graced the head and the foot of the stairs. All four were decorated with potted cacti.

The only thing which disturbed her was the matter of not finding the footprints which had been in the dust under the upper bedroom window. When she went to look for them they were gone and the floor had been wiped. The sunshine lay in a great bright square, and through it went the marks made by some kind of cloth swung in a semicircle through the dust.

Miss Rachel got a queer sense of being an intruder; the room had assumed an air of occupancy, of useful and secret purpose which must be kept from her.

She went out and closed the door. The bed, the dressing table, and the fire tongs she had had placed in a smaller front bedroom; she peeped in at them now, and their unfamiliarity dismayed her. She decided to unpack her largest suitcase, into which had gone bedding, and to make up the bed.

The immaculate pillow and the blue patchwork quilt improved the bed, but there was nothing to be done about the dressing table. It stood against the greenish wallpaper and looked sad. In the watery depths of its mirror Miss Rachel caught sight of herself.

Miss Rachel decided that a cup of hot tea would do her no harm. She went downstairs and into the kitchen and investigated the spigots of an ancient stove. The gasman had evidently been around, for there was gas in the pipes. She tried the faucet above the sink and it gave water. Feeling slightly more cheerful, she took her kettle from her little box of kitchen stuff and put it on full of water. She recalled a small grocery store a few blocks up the street and decided to go there for supplies, tea included.

Her purse and hat were in the living room. She was there, standing in front of an uncurtained window in lieu of a mirror, putting on her hat, when she discovered that she was about to have a caller. Someone was coming up the front walk toward the porch.

When Miss Rachel answered the bell she found herself face to face with a little old lady of approximately her own age.

"I'm Mrs. Ruddick. I live next door here." She nodded in the direction of the house toward the left whose occupants until now had been unknown to Miss Rachel. "I thought I'd better call on our new neighbor." She advanced toward the door.

This extreme of neighborliness in calling before the new arrival could possibly be settled annoyed Miss Rachel, as well as did an odd detail in the little old woman's appearance. Though Mrs. Ruddick was properly aged in her features and unusually bowed in her posture her hair was tinted a foolishly youthful yellow. It gave the effect of a golden halo in the shade of the porch, from under which she looked upon Miss Rachel with a mingling of wariness and charm.

Miss Rachel found herself saying automatically: "Won't you come in? I'm Miss Murdock."

Mrs. Ruddick came in and glanced about the hall and found something at once interesting about the little table at the foot of the stairs. "You like cactus, don't you?" She studied Miss Rachel brightly. "I do too. I have quite a few in my garden. I'll have to show them to you."

Miss Rachel ushered her into the living room.

Mrs. Ruddick stopped in the middle of the floor and stared about her. "Is this all you have? Oh, I didn't mean to sound rude, but you . . . ah . . . you know . . ." Her voice trailed away, and she watched Miss Rachel.

"I know it isn't much for the size of the room," Miss Rachel said smoothly. "I'll have to pick up a few more things before the place will seem livable."

Mrs. Ruddick edged herself into a rocker. She was dressed in crisp pink gingham with a white pinafore apron over her dress.

Were it not for the tinted hair, she would have made a picture of daintily aged femininity. A blue brooch sparkled in the bosom of the pinafore and caught Miss Rachel's eye. She was to have occasion to remember it later.

"I suppose you're wondering who your neighbors are," Mrs. Ruddick suggested archly.

Miss Rachel admitted to a slight curiosity about them the while she sat down and carefully removed her hat.

Mrs. Ruddick's eyes dwelt on the hat, but she tore them away. "If you've seen a child about it's Claudia. She lives on your other side. She's my great-granddaughter."

Miss Rachel must have shown some interest, for Mrs. Ruddick hurried on with pleasure. "Claudia's father married my granddaughter Annie. She was awfully young. Just sixteen. They ran away. Then she died just a year later when Claudia was born. You can imagine what a shock it was—my daughter'd scarcely got over the marriage when it seemed her Annie was dead, and they never gave her any satisfaction with Claudia, the Byerses didn't. They don't now. They keep her away, keep her strange with us. I don't think it's natural." She waited, as if hoping for Miss Rachel's agreement.

"And Claudia's grandparents?" Miss Rachel, no longer concealing her interest, nodded toward the windows.

Mrs. Ruddick smiled grimly. "The three of us live alone—at least, it has seemed alone these last eight years since Annie left us. There's my daughter Judith. Mrs. Hayes, that is. And her husband Bill. Neither of them ever got over what happened to Annie."

Miss Rachel murmured her regret at the thought of the young wife dying in childbirth.

"Childbirth, nothing." Mrs. Ruddick's forced charm had

vanished into snappishness. "It was the Byerses and the Tellinghams did it; I don't care what the doctor told us. It was Ronald Byers and that Tellingham woman. Alma." She spat the name. "It was their spooning and sparking and him running to Alma's house and Alma sneaking over to his. They lived here, mind you, and our Annie could look across her garden and see that woman out in the yard as if decent sunlight shouldn't scorch her. Oh, it—it—" She moved jerkily in her chair. "It makes my blood boil even yet. Even after eight years with Annie dead."

Miss Rachel was at a loss for words. She remembered Claudia's talk about her father having been engaged to Alma Tellingham before he had married her mother. The triangle of houses had contained another triangle, then, a human one full of the possibilities of hatred and revenge. There was no need to look into Mrs. Ruddick's eyes to know what lay there.

And this, Miss Rachel's house, had been Annie Byers' while she was married.

It was at this moment that Samantha, the cat, took it into her head to start yowling from the head of the stairs.

Mrs. Ruddick jumped, and all her color left her. "Heavens! What's that?"

Miss Rachel went to the hall door and called softly. Samantha, who was the color of marmalade, drifted down regally to join them. She stood in the living room to look at Mrs. Ruddick and then carefully circled Mrs. Ruddick's feet to reach the empty rocker.

"I guess she doesn't like me," Mrs. Ruddick said, watching Samantha's progress. "I can't say I'm fond of cats much, either. Maybe she senses it."

"Perhaps."

Mrs. Ruddick sat for a moment in silence while her mind worked. Then: "Have you seen Claudia?"

"I believe I saw her yesterday when I came to look at the house."

"I expect she was playing in the garden at the back. She's queer that way. She'd rather be alone than with people, especially than with us, though I can't blame her. It's her father and his sister and Grandpa Byers—I don't doubt they've turned her against us."

Miss Rachel kept her eyes on Samantha. "Surely they wouldn't do that?"

"Wouldn't they, though! It's their conscience, that's what it is. They know they killed that child's mother and they think to keep her away from us to keep her from knowing the truth."

Miss Rachel smoothed her skirt gently. "She seemed a very normal child to me."

Mrs. Ruddick shook her head. "Plays with toads! Imagine."

Miss Rachel kept discreet silence. Samantha yawned at Mrs. Ruddick.

"It isn't as if we haven't been nice to her or to them," Mrs. Ruddick went on. "My daughter bakes cakes for them; she sews for Claudia; she buys the child shoes. And are the cakes ever mentioned? Is she ever thanked for the clothes? Not on your life. It's take all and give nothing, not even a thank you, and for the life of me I can't see why Judith keeps on doing it. Especially with Bernice—that's Claudia's aunt—as snippy as you please and calling Claudia home if she thinks the child's so much as spoken to one of us."

"That seems cruel. Unnecessarily so," Miss Rachel put in.

"Cruel is no word for them, miss, nor for the way they treated our Annie." Mrs. Ruddick's voice snarled with the stress of her feeling, and for several moments she rocked backward and forward in silence, a faint squeak of the chair being the only sound in the room. The yellow hair swung in and out of the light from the window, and the blue stone in her brooch winked with brightness. "It's no word for them," she concluded at last, and then: "Perhaps I shouldn't have told you all our quarrel so soon. Maybe I should have waited and let you see them and know them; that's what I did before. Then the folks who rented here wouldn't believe when I did tell them." She lapsed again into silence. "They wouldn't believe the Byerses were all wrong the way they really are."

Miss Rachel was sorting things in her mind, classifying the people in the three houses according to their relationships with each other. There were Claudia, Ronald Byers, Bernice Byers, Grandpa Byers. They lived in the house to her right. To her left were Claudia's dead mother's people: Mrs. Ruddick, Mr. and Mrs. Hayes. And across the weedy garden lived the woman Claudia's father had almost married. Alma. Alma, her mother, their maid with the Slavic cheekbones. Just what, she wondered, had kept Ronald Byers from marrying Alma Tellingham, since his wife was dead eight years?

She glanced across at Mrs. Ruddick, the question on the tip of her tongue, and then stopped.

Mrs. Ruddick was crying.

Even as Miss Rachel glanced at her she began to speak. "I was with Annie when she died, miss. I'll never forget that child's face, nor her eyes, her poor beseeching eyes that wanted so to live." She bent forward and put her face into her hands. "Oh, miss, how it all comes back to me! Our little Annie and those wicked people. . . ." She quivered, and sobs racked her.

Miss Rachel went and knelt beside her and tried comforting words. She felt a sense of confusion. So much family history and so much emotion had been pushed at her, all in a chunk, that she had had no time to evaluate, to weigh them. She patted Mrs. Ruddick's shaking arm and wished for something of definite worth with which to console her.

Mrs. Ruddick eventually raised up and looked at her. "And you won't be taken in by their lies, will you now?" she asked earnestly.

"I—I don't suppose I'll even so much as hear them," Miss Rachel answered. "I haven't met Claudia's people, you see."

"You'll meet them," Mrs. Ruddick put in. "Promise me you won't believe what they tell you."

"I won't be fooled by something which isn't true," Miss Rachel decided. "I promise you that."

An undefined expression flickered in Mrs. Ruddick's eyes before she suppressed it. She began to wipe her cheeks with a handkerchief from her pinafore pocket, and then, as Miss Rachel drew away, belatedly she noticed the hat.

"Oh, I'll wager you were going out, and I've kept you all this time!" she cried. "Well, I'll run along now. Do come over real soon. Come see my cactus garden, won't you?" She rose heavily from the chair.

Miss Rachel put on her hat. "Yes, I'll come."

Mrs. Ruddick fumbled with her bosom absently, dropped her handkerchief, and stooped to retrieve it. "Were you going to market?"

"Yes, I was."

"You'll have quite a little walk. It's about three blocks up the street."

"I shan't mind."

Miss Rachel allowed Mrs. Ruddick to go out ahead of her and parted from her at the gate.

What with the walk and with shopping, it was a good half-hour before Miss Rachel returned to her house, burdened with groceries and with a mind set on the kettle, which she had forgotten. She entered the front door to find Samantha in the hall with her tail a-switch and her angry eyes fixed upon something in the living room.

The singing of the kettle, the sizzle of spurting water, reached her from the kitchen, and she made haste.

She almost tripped over Samantha, and the cat spat at her. The little box of tea fell out of the top of her bag. There was a jerky, nearly inaudible sound from beyond the open doorway.

Miss Rachel stopped to stare.

In the living room, stock-still and livid with a mixture of defiance and embarrassment, stood Mrs. Ruddick.

CHAPTER THREE

MRS. RUDDICK put out a hand to touch one of the rockers, as if for support, and she began to force herself to smile, "Miss—um—Murdock, I hope you'll excuse me running into your house. I thought I remembered having it on in here, and when I missed it at home I thought I'd just duck in and get it without troubling you." Her eyes made a sketchy search of the floor. "My brooch. I guess I haven't told you. It's my best brooch, and I've lost it."

Miss Rachel recalled the wink of blue light upon the bosom of Mrs. Ruddick's pinafore apron.

"It isn't that it's worth anything, but I've had it a long while and it was given me by a dear friend just before she died, and of course I mustn't lose it."

She ventured a look at Miss Rachel. Miss Rachel put her parcels into a chair.

As if in a hurry lest Miss Rachel offer to help her, she dropped to her knees and studied the undersides of the furniture. "I remembered you'd gone to market and I thought I'd just—" She pounced, flattening her hand against a tread of the rocker. "Here. I've found it. Now everything's all right. See?" She showed Miss Rachel the pin on an open palm.

Miss Rachel had a very good look at the brooch this time. The blue center stone was like a deep-set little eye—glass, obviously, but somehow awake and watchful in its frame of bubbly imitation pearls.

"Isn't it pretty?" Mrs. Ruddick chortled.

Miss Rachel couldn't decide whether she had just witnessed an honest discovery or a clever bit of legerdemain.

"It's a very interesting brooch," she said to Mrs. Ruddick's gratification. "I can't ever remember seeing one exactly like it."

Mrs. Ruddick snapped the pin into place with a half frown of concentration. "It was given me by Barbara Tellingham, practically on her deathbed."

"Tellingham?" Miss Rachel echoed. "But isn't that—?"

"Yes. That Alma wears the name, and believe me, she's a disgrace to it and her mother's no better, even if she was Barbara's daughter-in-law and Barbara was my school-days' chum. I can't like them, not even for Barbara's sake."

Miss Rachel shook her head. "It's unfortunate. How long has Barbara Tellingham been dead?"

"Barbara? Oh, ten years now. Ten years in April, that is. She died while Ronald was still engaged to Alma, long before he married our Annie. That's why she left things the way she did. The engagement, you see. It—"

There was a loud, firm knocking on the front door.

Miss Rachel opened the door upon a military-looking woman with red hair and a long sallow face.

"Is my mother, Mrs. Ruddick, with you?"

There was no attempt at a smile, no shade of friendliness in the prominent light blue eyes. Miss Rachel started to invite her in and then decided the circumstances didn't quite call for it.

"Coming, Judith!" Mrs. Ruddick came out of the living room in a hurry. "Is it luncheon, dear?"

"You're needed at home," her daughter said crisply. "Good day," she said to Miss Rachel.

"Don't mind Judith," Mrs. Ruddick said in a wheezing breath, going past. "She's been so broken up since Annie died."

Miss Rachel shut the door gently on Mrs. Ruddick's conciliatory smile and went into the kitchen to make sure that the kettle wasn't boiled dry. Claudia startled her by rattling the knob of the kitchen door. Miss Rachel let her in and was offered the squeezed remains of a cooky.

"It's for your lunch. Grandpa baked them. He fusses around in our kitchen when Aunt Bernice lets him. He made my birthday cake. I had a birthday day before yesterday. I was eight."

"Eight years old is quite grown up," Miss Rachel said thoughtfully. "Did you have a birthday party?"

"Just Grandpa and Aunt Bernice and Daddy. Me too. I blew out the candles, but it took two puffs."

Miss Rachel replenished the kettle and went back to the living room for her bag of groceries. Claudia tagged her, staring about at the interior of the house.

In the living room Samantha was on the floor playing with something under the edge of the radio. When she caught sight of Claudia she jumped into a chair and arched her back.

"Is he mad at me?" Claudia wondered.

"No, she's being friendly. She wants you to pet her."

Claudia stroked the cat with a cautious hand. "You're a lady cat, aren't you? What's your name?"

"Her name is Samantha, and she's as old as you are."

"Then she's grown up too. Does she have babies?"

"Only once," Miss Rachel remembered. The tea fell out of the bag to the floor as Miss Rachel straightened. "Oh, pick up my tea, will you?"

Claudia stooped as if for the tea, then scrambled in the direction of the radio. "Look, there's something shining." From under the radio she drew forth Mrs. Ruddick's pin. "Oh, I know what this is. It's my grandma's brooch. How do you suppose it came here?"

Miss Rachel decided privately that Mrs. Ruddick herself had most likely left it, hoping to make another entry in search of it when the house was empty.

She pressed it back into Claudia's offering hand. "Run next door and return it. I'm sure your grandmother will want it."

"Oh, I couldn't go there." Claudia drew back, her eyes wide on Miss Rachel. "I'm not allowed at Grandma Hayes' house. You see, Aunt Bernice and Grandpa and Daddy would be cross."

Miss Rachel stared in such surprise that Claudia blushed, fumbled the brooch, and dropped it. "Well, I guess I'd better tell you. Daddy says that Grandma Ruddick caused all our troubles. He says she talks too much and that she doesn't get things straight, and a long time ago she said something about Daddy that wasn't true and that changed everything for him. That's why I can't go next door, not ever. Not even when you've asked me."

Miss Rachel took the brooch from the pink palm. "It's quite all right, dear. Take the tea to the kitchen, and I'll bring these other things. Do you suppose you could have a bite with me?"

She dropped the brooch into the bag, and when she peeped in at it, it was slipped down between the bread and the box of sugar cubes, a blue eye set in bubbles.

And then she forgot it.

She and Claudia had watercress sandwiches and tea, and the man came to turn on the electricity, and another man came in a limousine to ask for the elder Mr. Byers. The big car bore a company's name, something about aircraft. Miss Rachel sent him next door.

After lunch Miss Rachel and Claudia made an inspection of the garden. It badly needed weeding. Claudia offered the suggestion that there might be some gardening tools in the cellar.

Miss Rachel located the cellar door in a pantry off the kitchen and looked down into gloom. She wished suddenly that she could have seen the cellar first with the rental agent pointing out its nice features. Halfway down was a loose step, and Miss Rachel almost fell. Putting out a hand to save herself, she caught what looked to be a timber set firmly in the wall, and it came away with unexpected suddenness and clattered down ahead of her.

She teetered, almost toppling, with Claudia pulling her skirts from behind. When she was sure of her balance she looked again at the spot on the wall. It was fogged with cobwebs, shadowed by the low roof of the stairs, but Miss Rachel saw that there was quite a space inside and that there was something in it. A black box. A box with a cold metallic feel.

Under Claudia's wondering stare she took it out.

The catch flew apart under her touch, and she lifted the lid. She felt some how like an interloper and had to remind herself that, after all, since she had rented the house she was privileged to explore it and to open such hidden boxes as she might find. From the box she took forth two letters, both addressed to Mr. Ronald Byers, the date stamps reading September 1934.

"Just letters?" Claudia asked disappointedly.

Almost without thought Miss Rachel slipped one letter out

of its envelope and began to read. The words, the tone of it, brought her up short.

RONNIE, MY DEAR:

It is much too late to try to explain; too late, too, for you to understand what I feel—my abasement and agony. Death is so final, so complete, such an utter end of everything. There is now no way that I can talk to Annie . . .

Miss Rachel put the letter into the envelope with a feeling of having violated the privacy of the person who had written it, and as she did so the two pages dropped apart and the signature of the writer shone black and small at the bottom of the second page. *Alma.* The Tellingham girl, the girl Ronald Byers had been about to marry just before he married Claudia's mother. Miss Rachel slipped the two letters into the box. She had a sinking, funny sensation inside her, as though the walls about her were taking on new and terrifying possibilities.

Claudia tugged her skirt. "Was it something important?"

Miss Rachel looked down at the box and wondered what to do with it. At last, Claudia having promised to keep the secret, she put it back into its hole and retrieved the piece of wood which had covered the opening.

They went down to the cellar floor, but Miss Rachel's mind was far from the subject of gardening tools. Her thoughts were busy with the letters, with whether Ronald Byers had put them where they were and, if so, why. There had been a great many cobwebs about and over the piece of lumber which had fallen, and the box had had on it a thick layer of dust. Had Ronald Byers put away Alma's letters when his young wife died, never looked at them again, never contacted Alma or listened to what she had to say?

"Here's something we could use," Claudia offered. She had gone to a shelf under the windows and was lifting a long piece of iron—a file, heavily rusted, that sagged in her small grip. "We could dig with this, sort of. Couldn't we?"

The odor of the cellar was damp and earthy, and the sight of the thing in Claudia's unsteady hands sent a little shiver of cold up Miss Rachel's back. "Put it down," she cried, and at Claudia's look of surprise: "You might drop it and hurt yourself."

"Couldn't we use it in the garden?"

"No, it isn't what we need. We need grass clippers and a little hoe to cut the weeds. A trowel to loosen the dirt. But not that."

Claudia put down the file with some reluctance. "There isn't anything else at all."

In a far corner stood the furnace, like a spider with thick up-ended legs. Against one wall was laundry equipment: two tubs and a built-in bin and a small shelf with an empty bottle on it which had once contained bluing. As Claudia had said, there was nothing which resembled a tool.

"I'll have to buy the things we need," Miss Rachel decided. "Let's go back upstairs."

They went up and out into the yard, and Claudia helped at pulling up some of the larger weeds by the roots. While they worked and the afternoon sun warmed them and the earth Miss Rachel was conscious of comings and goings from the other houses. A short bald-headed man, stoop-shouldered and with an expression of half hearted surprise, came out of the Hayes house and watched them while he clipped a hedge.

"That's Grandpa Hayes," Claudia informed Miss Rachel.

"He's henpecked. Daddy says he's double henpecked 'cause he has Grandma Hayes and Grandma Ruddick both telling him what to do and what not to do. Daddy says when he wants to go to bed he has to ask Grandma Hayes, and when he wants to get up he has to ask Grandma Ruddick. You know, he was my mama's daddy." She slid a look at him from under Miss Rachel's tugging arms. "He gives me candy sometimes."

Miss Rachel looked at the little man, and he ducked his head and set the clippers flying.

The Slavic-faced woman came out upon the rear porch across the alley, but this time she did not stay to watch. She shook out a small rug and went inside, and Miss Rachel noted that the little man in the next yard neither looked at her nor glanced up at the sharp slam of the door.

Neither did he display any interest when a smart coupé drew into the drive and stood purring by the door through which the Slavic woman had gone. A tall young woman got out from the driver's seat. She was in sport clothes, a tan coat with a blue sweater and skirt beneath it, a small dark felt crushed down over black curling hair. She looked briefly in Miss Rachel's direction before going to the other side of the car and opening the door for an older woman. In that brief glimpse Miss Rachel saw that she was quite undeniably beautiful. Twenty-seven or -eight, and the black hair a frame for an oval face with a soft, well-shaped mouth, wide dark eyes, and brows like a little line made with a brush.

The woman she assisted from the other side of the car was as tall as the girl but not so straight, and the hair under her severe hat was gray, cut short and neatly waved. Her face was narrower, its expression petulant. When she had gone into the house the girl put the car into the garage.

During the time that the car stood by the back door across the alley Mr. Hayes put away his clippers and disappeared inside.

It was much later in the afternoon before there was any sign of life from Claudia's home. Then a woman of about thirty-two or -three came out and called, and when she saw Miss Rachel she introduced herself as Bernice Byers.

"I hope Claudia hasn't made a nuisance of herself." She studied Claudia's grubby dress critically. "I'm afraid she's not much of a help. Most of the time she simply gets herself dirty and makes trouble for everyone."

"She's been a great deal of company for me," Miss Rachel said.

Bernice Byers slid her an odd glance. "You mustn't believe all that Claudia tells you. She's rather a little gossip when she gets started and finds that someone will listen. Claudia, come home now."

Miss Rachel saw what was in Bernice Byers' mind. She felt an urge to defend Claudia on the score of gossiping, since Mrs. Ruddick had so far outdone her in that direction, but repressed the desire for the sake of tact.

Bernice was an efficient-looking woman, but there was an almost deliberate plainness about her, from the short, center-parted brown bob to the sensible oxfords on her feet. She was the sort of woman Miss Rachel classifies as a spiritual old maid, born to be practical and to prick such bubbles of fancy as others try to blow. When Claudia went to her she made a long ceremony of brushing the dress and of wiping the shoes with a bit of grass, and Miss Rachel experienced a feeling of guilt for having encouraged the child to help her.

"Next time you wish to help Miss Murdock come get one

of Grandpa's tools," Bernice said severely. "Then you won't get quite as soiled as you do in using your hands."

They went into their house, and Miss Rachel gave over pulling weeds. She was tired, and now that the day had definitely begun to wane she was getting uneasy. She had a vision of Jennifer at supper, served with Mrs. Marble's sumptuous cooking, lonely and puzzled because Rachel had taken it into her head to go away on a wild-goose chase. Tonight was the night for creamed chicken and Southern biscuits with quince butter. It was also about the time of month that Mrs. Perley was apt to call. Mrs. Perley was a policeman's widow, much cherished by Miss Rachel for her fund of criminal narratives.

The thought of missing Mrs. Perley so vexed Miss Rachel that she went inside and busied herself with preparations for dinner. It was by now almost sundown, and the walls of the kitchen were red with the dark, reflected glow. Miss Rachel opened a little can of peas and put a lamb chop into a skillet over a brisk fire. She decided against having any more tea and brewed a little panful of coffee with the idea that it might help to keep her awake.

The sun went down while she was eating, and the long twilight set in. Washing her dishes, she could look out into the garden, across the alley to the house of the Tellinghams. The tall girl with the black curling hair must be Alma. How much, Miss Rachel wondered, had Alma Tellingham actually had to do with the heartbreak and death of young Annie Byers? Was the letter in the box in the cellar a confession of guilt, a crying out of repentance at her hand in the young wife's death?

A black shadow crossed the pane of the Tellinghams' back door. The stocky figure of the Slavic woman, Miss Rachel thought. There was a light on in the second story, also, and pale curtains blowing out from under the glass.

It was almost night now, and for a moment Miss Rachel's hand started for the electric switch. Then she thought to herself that she'd just leave the dishes where they were, dried and stacked on the sink, and go into the living room and try for a good program on the radio. She went through the small passage into the hall. It was quite dark here, though a narrow window on either side of the front door let in a faint light from the street lamp outside. The stairway, going up to the left, looked spidery and graceful in the dense gloom. The panel of the door into the living room shone faintly; the door was ajar, and as Miss Rachel looked at it Samantha's green eyes glowed suddenly and near the floor.

It was at that instant that Miss Rachel realized that a part of what she had expected of this house was coming true.

Soft but distinct came the sounds of someone walking about on the floor above.

Miss Rachel went to the stairs and searched out the banister and put a hand on it.

A door creaked softly; there was a minute of complete silence and darkness, and then, incredibly, Miss Rachel found herself looking up at a lighted candle and a pair of eyes and a gun.

CHAPTER FOUR

A VOICE barked down at her, a man's voice full of a kind of wary anger. "Who's there? Speak up, whoever you are." And he lifted the gun a little.

Miss Rachel experimented with her vocal chords, "I—I'm Miss M-Murdock," she managed.

"What the hell are you doing here?" He was at the top step now, and the barrel of his pistol shone in the candlelight.

"I'm just—just staying here," she said, very small.

He came down about three steps and lowered the candle and the gun. "Oh," he said suddenly. He had undoubtedly seen what a very small and elderly lady Miss Rachel really was. "Are you looking for someone?"

"No."

A puzzled expression came into his eyes, and Miss Rachel was reminded all at once of Claudia, of Claudia coming up from under the radio with Mrs. Ruddick's brooch in her hand. The eyes, Miss Rachel thought, are the same. Wideset, somehow fearless. "Are you Claudia's father?" she hazarded.

"Claudia? Is something wrong with Claudia?" He ran lightly down the rest of the steps to where Miss Rachel stood. "Don't tell me there's been an accident!'

"No. You see, I've met Claudia, and you look like her, and so I thought you might be Mr. Byers."

The look of puzzlement increased. "Wait. Will you tell me how you came to follow me into this house?"

"But I didn't follow you. I was here. I've been here all day."

A slow flush crept into his face, and acute embarrassment showed in his eyes. "Of course. I'd forgotten. It's been vacant for so long. You've rented the house, haven't you?"

"Yes. I moved in during the morning."

"And I haven't been home yet this evening, and so I didn't know." He paused for an instant, and Miss Rachel wondered whether he might not be going to explain why he had come into a supposedly dark and empty house with a candle and a revolver. Instead, he said briskly: "I'm afraid I've been guilty of the worst sort of trespassing. If there had been a light I'd have guessed that the place was rented again. All I can do is to apologize from the bottom of my heart and hope that I haven't frightened you too much."

He looked suddenly like Claudia then, like Claudia when she was being scolded by her aunt Bernice for getting dirty.

"It's quite all right," Miss Rachel said. She felt the contagion of his embarrassment. "I suppose you—ah—are more or less in the habit of keeping track of things here."

As though to seize on the suggestion, he said quickly: "Yes, that's right. You see, the house is part of an estate. It's not mine, but I've kept an eye on it. There's the possibility of fire. If it went the other houses might go. Then—it's best to discourage prowlers." He looked about at the gloom beyond the candlelight, and Miss Rachel got the impression that he was thinking of something more than a fire or a vagrant; and she remembered his background in relation to this house, his sudden marriage, his life here with a girl of sixteen, his (according to Mrs. Ruddick) continued affair with Alma Tellingham, his widowerhood when Annie had died.

Some of all this had left its mark in him. He was fine-drawn for a young man. When he frowned in concentration his brows drew down hard and thick as though frowning were an old art with him, and his smile was a brief lightening of a habitual grimness.

"Are your lights working?" he asked. Before Miss Rachel could answer he strode off toward the front door and pushed the switch, and the hall sprang into bright relief. He blew out the candle quickly and thrust it into the pocket of his coat. He must have put the gun away on his walk to the door; there was no sign of it now.

He went back to the foot of the steps and hesitated there. He did not look at Miss Rachel. "I wonder if I've left anything upstairs. I can't remember. Perhaps I'd better look."

He started up, and Miss Rachel started up after him. He stopped and looked back; and as though he had said it, Miss Rachel knew that he wanted to go upstairs alone. He *had* left something there and he *did* recall it. A sudden determination came over Miss Rachel not to let him get away with it. He had barged into her house and held a gun on her and frightened her out of her wits with his silly candle, and now, by heaven, she was going to find out as much as she could of his reason for being there.

But he went no further. He stood there and looked at the little old lady on the steps below and frowned and said he guessed there was nothing he'd left after all, and almost before Miss Rachel knew it he had said good night and was gone. The door clicked shut after him, and his steps went off the porch into silence.

The narrow windows on either side of the door were neither frosted nor curtained, so that Miss Rachel knew he had a perfect way of seeing what she did if he had stayed to watch. She took a moment to turn out the light, then scurried upstairs as fast as she could.

She took the four bedrooms and bath clockwise fashion, beginning with the door to her left, which was her own bedroom. She pulled the shades before turning on the lights; it took no more than a glance into each room to show it empty. In the last room, the room that overlooked the garden and the windows of the Tellingham house, she found a much-increased darkness, and when she had felt her way to the window and touched the sill something teetered off and fell with a crash.

Miss Rachel made haste to the light switch without waiting to pull the blind.

Under the window were the remains of a saucer. The pane had been covered with an oblong of black heavy cloth tacked with thumbtacks at the top and the sides. And the rest of the room was bare as usual.

Miss Rachel examined the saucer and found in it a great deal of dropped wax. It had been Ronald Byers' candleholder, obviously. From the amount of wax in the saucer and the number of blobs on the floor, Miss Rachel judged that more than one candle had been used, that whatever Byers had been doing in this room had required some time. She took a moment to investigate the closet. On a shelf above eye level she felt out a package of thumbtacks and an extra candle. Ronald Byers had not brought his candle and his black cloth with him then; he had kept them here in the closet.

Miss Rachel went out into the room and stood quiet and tried to figure out what Byers could have been doing.

The candles were explained by the fact of there having been no electricity in the deserted house; the black cloth insured secrecy. But what else? Why a lighted, secret room which was utterly bare? What could he have been doing here which required not so much as a pen and a bottle of ink? Not even a chair to sit in?

Miss Rachel went to the black cloth and inspected it. It was not one cloth but three, close-woven cotton broadcloth pinned together at the corners with safety pins. She bent, lifted the bottom edge, and peeped through. On a line with her eyes was the upper window of the Tellingham house, the one lighted pane she had seen with its curtains blowing from under. She watched a moment, and something very odd took place. The light in the Tellingham window went out and came on again, twice and very quickly. Miss Rachel dropped the black cloth. She was afraid she might have been seen. She put out the light in the room and went out to the top of the stairs.

The hallway below was dark and quiet, and its odors drifted up about Miss Rachel on the landing. Mingling with the smell of old wallpaper and dust was the stale aroma of fried lamb chops from the kitchen. She had, then, left the connecting door open, and she would be plagued by the kitchen smell all over the house unless she closed it.

She went down carefully in the dark, the long rail of the banister shining faintly ahead of her. From the living room Samantha greeted her with a faint mewing. At the little passageway into the kitchen she found the knob of the door and began to close it. A sudden idea came into her head that she should have turned on the hall light; there was no sense, really, in this walking about in the dark. Ronald Byers had long since gone home, and he probably had had little interest, in the first place, in what noncommittal articles he had left in her house. There was nothing to be deduced from them beyond the fact of his being here, and she had discovered that in the beginning.

She was pulling the door toward her when a sudden shadow darkened the pane of the door that let out into the garden. The lights from the Tellingham house outlined the dark shape, the unmistakable roundness of a head and the breadth of arms and shoulders.

The latch in the kitchen scraped faintly; the reflected shape wavered darkly and advanced. Someone was coming in.

Miss Rachel felt suddenly that to meet another stranger in the dark was too much, quite more than she could endure, and she retreated swiftly to the hall way and the light switch. She clicked on the lights, and the hall showed bare and bright, the little table at the foot of the stairs bearing its potted cactus, Samantha sitting at the living-room door washing her fur with a meticulous tongue. Miss Rachel went back to the kitchen doorway.

The door to the garden was slightly ajar, swinging a little, but the shadow was gone from the pane, and when she peered out into the garden there seemed nothing to see but the lights of the Tellingham house across the alley and nothing to hear but the dry chirp of a cricket from beneath one of the rose bushes.

She went out upon the back steps and breathed the night air and tried to see more deeply into the dark.

A radio began to play in the Hayes house, and Mrs. Ruddick's voice sang out querulously from a back room, asking that it be tuned down. In the house to her right—Claudia's house, she called it to herself—a light burned in the kitchen. Miss Rachel waited. Bernice Byers came out upon the rear porch and scraped a dish briskly into the garbage pail and clanged the lid getting it back on and then spoke out sharply: "Father, what are you doing out in the yard?"

A man's voice replied in a soft mutter that Miss Rachel failed to catch.

Bernice said, "Well, you're like as not to catch your death of cold doing it. Set your gopher trap tomorrow. That's soon enough."

"The damned things dig at night," the man's voice complained.

Miss Rachel flattened against the screen as a bent shape went up the steps of Claudia's house. This would be Claudia's grandfather, Grandpa Byers. The light from the Byers kitchen gave Miss Rachel a glimpse of white hair, pale aged skin, palsied hands reaching for the latch.

Bernice said very quietly: "He won't meet her tonight. The house is rented."

"It won't be long before she'll have another place picked out." The old man tried to speak as softly as his daughter, but emotion roughened his voice. "She'll toll him away, and he'll listen to her. We ought to try talking to him about it."

"That wouldn't do, Father. Besides, there isn't really anything definite yet. If there were, Ronald would tell us."

The old man scraped his feet at the edge of the porch. "Ronald's getting ready to believe her. Wait and see. They'll be man and wife yet, one of these days."

Bernice put decision into her tone. "There's a great deal for Alma to explain before she gets into this house."

"I wish we had moved away years ago," the old man said querulously. "The ground is poor, won't grow anything, and all these eight years since Annie died I've had to work out under the eye of that spying foreign woman. She acts like Ronnie gave her the gate instead of her mistress."

"Perhaps we can think of some way to keep Ronald from seeing Alma," Bernice suggested. "Come inside."

Miss Rachel imagined that some sort of conference would now take place between Bernice and her father on the subject of keeping Alma Tellingham away from Ronald. The time element in the thing interested Miss Rachel. Some ten years ago Ronald and Alma had been sweethearts. Alma's grandmother, Barbara Tellingham, had died, leaving property in some way—Mrs. Ruddick had not explained how—which involved their being married. Then, and suddenly (this, too, according to Mrs. Ruddick), Ronald had married Annie Byers and had had a little over a year of marriage in this house which she had rented. Claudia had been born and Annie had died. And for eight years Alma Tellingham and Ronald Byers had made no move to renew their old romance.

Until now.

Had it taken eight years for the bitterness and the reproach to wear away? Had the blame for Annie's death stood between them so vividly that seeing each other was torture? What was it the hidden letter had said?—*my abasement and agony.* Did that mean what it seemed to, that Alma Tellingham had been overcome with shame for the way she had acted during the year of Annie's marriage, that she saw too late what she had done and craved such forgiveness as Ronald could give in Annie's name?

The radio had quieted in the Hayes house; the light was gone from the Byers kitchen. Across the alley, the Tellingham house, for all that its lights were lit, looked deserted and peaceful.

And yet, Miss Rachel thought, there must be a great deal

going on in these three houses, a great deal of worry and hatred and intrigue, of old scores being reckoned up and new plottings being hatched. Out in the garden, at this moment, reposed the remains of the toad that Claudia had loved, that some one who did not love Claudia had crushed to lifelessness and left for the child to find, and the white stone shining in the dark was a monument to more than a dead playmate.

It was a little beacon of things to come, a white shadow on very dark ground, a moment ticked off on someone's litany of horror.

Miss Rachel slipped into the house feeling very cold.

She went into the living room and put on the light and listened for a while to the radio. When the ten o'clock news was finished she went up to bed. Samantha went with her, and Miss Rachel, standing by the light switch in her gown, had a last look at the room.

The bed stood with its footboard facing the window. Against the wall by the closet door the dressing table showed a greenish reflection of the room. The fire tongs were against the upper bed leg, just under Miss Rachel's pillow. Samantha was curled, eyes half shut, her tail laid across her paws, ready for sleep. And there was nothing else in the room. Nothing at all.

Miss Rachel pushed the light switch, and the night came into the room as she felt her way to the bed.

She stared at it with her head on the pillow; stared at the dark and thought of Jennifer and their comfortable house with nothing in it save familiar and long-used things; remembered each room and the way it was furnished; and she could recall no time when she would have been afraid to get up in the night and go anywhere in her house, when she would have expected to see anything to frighten her or to have heard any sound except ordinary ones. And now she was afraid.

Not afraid enough to get up and dress and go home. But watchful. Tense. So nervous that she expected never that night to go to sleep.

But sleep she did, eventually, and perhaps much for the best. There was little she could have done to help what happened that night, and to have been awake would almost certainly have guaranteed her own death.

When she awoke the room was beginning to lighten with the dawn. She was cold under the small amount of bedding she had thought sufficient. There was a crick in her neck from lying with her head propped up by the overfat pillow that Jennifer had mistakenly packed instead of Miss Rachel's own. When she lifted her knees the cold air rushed in under the bedclothes and made her shiver. She sat up, pulled the covers up with her, and looked around.

The first thing she noticed was the absence of the cat. Samantha's usual way was to be at the foot of the bed, watching, ready to leap in the direction of the kitchen at the first sign of Miss Rachel's stirring. Miss Rachel put a hand down to touch the spot where Samantha had been curled. It was cold.

She looked toward the window, where the thin light came into the room from under the green blind, and then she glanced toward the dressing table and froze.

It was unbelievable, of course, the thing that sat there.

She rubbed her eyes, tried to rub it away before she accepted its actuality. She had seen it last in the cellar on the dusty shelf under the window, where Claudia had found it and had suggested its use as a garden tool. Now it leaned against the wall, made a triangle with its shadow on the greenish paper, the tapering point at the top and the blunt end against the floor.

It was the big iron file, of course, and its being in that particular place wouldn't have had any terrifying connotations except for what seemed to be on it and on the floor under it.

There were stains on the file, and something dark and viscid had dripped down and made a little pool around it.

CHAPTER FIVE

MISS RACHEL put out a hasty foot, touched the cold floor with her toes, remembered the underside of the bed, and jerked the foot back. She crouched inside a tent of bedcovers and stared at the file and waited. The silence had an early, eerie quality because there was as yet no stirring from out of doors. When it seemed to Miss Rachel that her ears would break from further listening she risked a quick look under the bed. The floor was empty.

She stared again at the file. The dark red stuff was blood, and, recalling the dead toad and Samantha's unusual absence, Miss Rachel had a sudden foretaste of grief. Samantha had been killed by the same callous fiend who had left the pet toad for Claudia to find. Miss Rachel's token was the bloody file, a more subtle clue for her adult mind. She grew suddenly very angry, slid out of bed, and began to dress with shaking hands.

She looked first through every room on the second floor and found them bare and innocent. She paused at the top of the stairs and looked down for a long minute, and for the first time she actually hated the house and hated herself for bringing her pet to its death. Samantha's death might be part of a pattern and

45

call for coolheaded logic, but all that she could feel now was a hot surge of tears. The memory of Claudia with her toad wasn't any help.

Miss Rachel went downstairs slowly, wiping her eyes.

There was nothing unusual about the living room, nor the two closed rooms which had once been the dining room and the library. They were—Miss Rachel sought for a word—religiously bare. On the dust of the window sill in the library Miss Rachel found a paw print, a souvenir of Samantha's prowling. It sent her hurrying to the back part of the house.

She was exploring the cupboard under the sink, expecting to find Samantha's mangled body momentarily, when there was a scratch and a yowl from the direction of the pantry.

Miss Rachel rocked back upon her heels and nearly fell, then scrambled up from her sitting position and opened the pantry door. Samantha limped through. She looked ruffled and angry. From the tip of one marmalade-colored ear hung a festoon of cobweb. Dust rose from her fur when Miss Rachel reached to stroke it. One hind leg was lame, and when Miss Rachel tried to touch it Samantha hissed at her.

But nowhere on Samantha was there any blood.

Miss Rachel left the cat sitting in the kitchen beginning the cleaning-up process and went into the pantry. Here were two walls of empty shelves, a box of old fruit jars, and the door to the cellar stairway, which was open.

She peered down into the semidarkness. She was still confused by the appearance of Samantha, alive, and her mind was just beginning to take up the new problem: what of the blood on the file? She could see from the top of the steps that the board which covered the hidden box was in place. The cellar seemed to be empty, though the corner which held the furnace was full of shadow.

She went back into the kitchen and unscrewed the light bulb there and brought it to the empty socket at the head of the cellar stairs. Snapped on, it gave out a sickly yellow glow that relieved the gloom but slightly. After a moment's struggle with herself she decided to go down.

The creaking of the stairs, loud in the otherwise complete stillness, set goose flesh creeping up her arms. When she paused the rest of the house seemed to wait; if a thing of timber and cement can be said to be holding its breath—that's what the house was doing. She had a sudden imaginary vision of the four bedrooms on the top floor, full of sunshine and emptiness, quiet, tuned like four big ears on the sound of her steps. She shook herself, put a foot on the cement floor, and said in a voice which surprised her: "Is anybody here?"

In the dead quiet which answered she had time to remember the ridiculous joke of the farmer at the chicken coop at night asking the same question, and if an African voice had answered, "Nawsuh, boss, ain't nobody here but us chickens," she would have accepted it, momentarily at least, as a fitting part of the fantastic dream she was living.

The silence came to an end with a hideous yowl from the kitchen. Miss Rachel ran up toward the sunny pantry with a sense of relief. She found Samantha tense, watching the kitchen door, and Claudia's alert face thrust in through the crack. It was perhaps the one time Samantha lived up to her reputation as a watchdog. Miss Rachel smiled.

"Come inside, dear."

If there is *something in the cellar*, she thought, it will have to wait. Bloody file or no bloody file, I'm not going to frighten Claudia.

"Have you had your breakfast?" Claudia wondered. "Not yet," said Miss Rachel.

"If you fix an extra slice of toast I'd eat it. There's nobody up yet at our house. I'm hungry too."

"Suppose I boil you an egg. Would you like that?"

So much success embarrassed Claudia, and she only nodded an acceptance of the egg. For some fifteen minutes Miss Rachel was busy with breakfast, and then, when the time had come to eat it, she found herself without any appetite. She was watching butter melt into her toast, feeling a dry constriction in her throat when Claudia suddenly looked up.

"You know my grandma Ruddick's pin?" When Miss Rachel seemed slow to understand she went on, "The blue one with the pearls that she wears on her front. Here." Claudia patted her diaphragm.

"Yes, I remember."

Claudia's look was direct. "Where is it?"

Miss Rachel's thought pulled free of a whirlpool into which the bloody file had been planted like a lodestone and tried to recall the whereabouts of the brooch. "The bag," she offered. "It's in the bag the groceries came in."

The bag still sat on the sink board with a few cans in it. Claudia got up to explore, took out the groceries, shook the paper sack upside down, stuck chin and nose and eyes in to stare. "It's gone," she decided. "Perhaps you put it away."

"I didn't take it out of the bag. It must have dropped somehow." Miss Rachel eyed the floor in a cursory examination.

Claudia went back to eating her egg. After a few minutes' silence she said, "Or you might have taken it down into the cellar."

Miss Rachel all but jumped. "The cellar?"

"When you were down there in the middle of the night."

Miss Rachel fixed on Claudia's expression, found in it nothing but a casual anxiety about the pin. "I wasn't in the cellar after dark," she said firmly. "Why did you think that I was?"

"I saw your light."

"My light?"

"Your *candle*light," Claudia elucidated.

"And you saw *me?*" Miss Rachel got out, wondering whether she had begun to walk in her sleep.

"No, not you." Claudia seemed on the verge of being amused. "Your little, flickering light."

Claudia had seen a light in the cellar; that much seemed certain. "What time?" Miss Rachel wondered.

"Oh, away in the night. Everybody was in bed, even over at Alma's, and I'd been asleep for a long time. I remember even the big street lamp down at the corner was out." She looked with a little bashfulness at the crumbs of egg on her plate. "You know, I thought maybe you'd be afraid and keep your lights on, the way I'd like to do sometimes, and so I went to the window and looked over. And sure enough—but of course a candle isn't as bad as a *big* light. Is it?"

"And how long," said Miss Rachel out of a dry throat, "did this candlelight stay in the cellar?"

"Not long," Claudia decided. "And it went upstairs?"

Claudia shook her head. "It went out, and then everything was dark." She stared curiously. "Don't you remember?"

Miss Rachel saw that it was best for Claudia's sake that she remember. "I thought I heard a noise and I went to look."

"And was it anything?"

"No. Nothing."

Claudia yawned politely. "We still haven't found Grandma Ruddick's pin."

"Perhaps it's been thrown outside accidentally. Would you like to look in the trash box?"

This wasn't the tidiest way of getting rid of Claudia; there would probably be repercussions from Aunt Bernice, but Miss Rachel was getting desperate. She had to get Claudia away; she had to explore the cellar before . . . Before what? Before she went mad wondering what candlelight, a file, a ruffled and injured cat, could possibly add up to?

Claudia went outside, and Miss Rachel was careful in latching the door. Then she went back through the pantry to the cellar stairs where the inadequate light bulb struggled in the gloom. Down below the dirty windows were letting in the sun a little, and a few imprisoned flies buzzed in the warmth.

She went down more slowly than before and first examined the space under the workbench and then the corner behind the furnace. There were cobwebs under the bench, a rat's nest behind the furnace. But in leaving the furnace she saw the door.

It had not occurred to her that the boxed-in space under the stairs was a closet, because she had not until now been far enough toward the corner directly beneath the stairs to see the door that let into it. The door faced, not the cellar itself, but the rear corner containing the furnace.

She walked over and took hold of the knob and turned it, but pulling had no effect. The thing was locked. She shook it a little, looked about on the floor, half expecting to find the key dropped there, and then bent and tried to see through the keyhole. Inside, if it was the inside she was seeing, was as black as midnight.

She tried smelling and succeeded in getting a choking amount of dust from the recesses of the lock.

She walked toward the stairs, measuring the closet with her eye. It was about nine feet at its widest point, next the floor. Only the fact that the stairs went up steeply allowed for the height of the door at the entry. She walked back, pulled again at the knob, stood in introspection, trying to recall any odd keys upstairs.

There was, far away and very soft, the sound of a door shutting.

The sound registered, and her mind accepted it before the full implication burst on her. Both the front and the back doors were locked. If there were someone inside he had gotten in by illegitimate means, and she had better see who it was. And she had, too, a queer aversion to being discovered near the closet until she knew what was in it.

So she went back upstairs.

Samantha was gone from the kitchen, and Claudia had disappeared from the yard. She could see the trash box by putting a hand on the sink and leaning into the window. The garden looked sunny and alive, full of pushing weeds and insects, the dew sparkling when the wind moved through. Another, a blue sparkle caught her eye, and she glanced down. On the sink beside her fingers was Mrs. Ruddick's brooch.

It *had* been in the trash box, and Claudia had brought it in.

But, no, for the back door was fastened; she herself had latched it.

She tried the back door, and it was locked. She hurried through the passage into the hall and tried the big front door between its two narrow windows. The only way that it could have been opened from outside would have been with a key, and Claudia had had none.

Samantha cried from behind her, and she turned. At the top of the steps stood the cat. The animal was angry, her tail rigid and bushy, her eyes afire.

It was seeing Samantha which convinced Miss Rachel that there was, or had been, a prowler in the house.

She went through the upper bedrooms hurriedly and found them as before, even to the bloody file, by now rapidly drying, and the odd black-out arrangement at the window which faced the Tellingham house. The lower floor was as empty. The sound she had heard from the cellar had been departure.

There was a rusted key in the kitchen lock, a lock not used because of the more modern night latch which had been installed above. Miss Rachel took the key and went back to the cellar. Now, she thought, it's time to quit dillying and dallying. She tried thrusting the key into the cellar-closet keyhole.

"There'll be nothing inside but tools," she said half aloud. Her mind was set firmly against the possibility of finding anything unpleasant. It was bad enough having heard a prowler, having your cat frightened, having a silly blue pin disappear and then reappear again as though it had legs to walk about with. . . . She paused on the memory of the pin. Was there a connection between the reappearance of the pin and the slipping in of the prowler whose departure she had just heard?

And speaking of slipping in—who had slipped the bloody file into her room, and for what reason?

The key would go so far in the lock, but not far enough. Miss Rachel prodded, while her mind kept busy with the puzzle of the file, the blue brooch, the prowler who sought her house by night and by day as casually as though it were his own. There was, she was sure, something plugging up the keyhole.

With a bent hairpin she fished for the obstruction.

It came eventually, a little wad of white material, soiled, hemmed on one edge, creases in it as though it had been part of a pleated ruffle. Miss Rachel dropped it and went back to work with the key.

The lock was stubborn; the key inclined to stick in a side-wise position. Drawing the key out on one of her frequent attempts to get it set correctly, she found a yellow hair wound on the shank.

The hair annoyed Miss Rachel. It seemed a picayune and unnecessary nuisance. She picked it off and let it fall, but she was to recall it later. Like the white stone over the toad, it was a breath out of the hurricane to come.

Just now she was interested in the final yielding of the lock.

The bolts groaned and the key let out a shriek, but when she turned the knob and pulled it the door began to open. In her expectancy Miss Rachel jumped erect and pulled it wide.

The light spread into the closet in a fanwise beam, and there was indeed a clutter of tools just by the door, small stuff covered with rust and cobwebs, a trowel and a claw-shaped digging tool and grass shears and a wrench.

And there was, also, an odd bundle of stuff pushed back into the corner under the stairs. Miss Rachel peered, stepped in, and bent over in shadow.

It looked like clothing, jumbled and tossed in to be out of the way. She put out a hand and pulled a bit of it down.

For a long moment she stood perfectly quiet, full of her own heart's terrific beating and the sudden deadness of her arms and legs. She hadn't expected this horror, and looking at it didn't quite bring belief. It couldn't be real, this travesty of Mrs. Ruddick in her pinafore, the contorted body so vivid a contrast to Mrs. Ruddick's normal torpidity. From the shadow Mrs. Ruddick gazed back from a head which by no stretch of the imagination could still have life in it. Her legs were far under, her arms tightly back. A stub of candle lay by her hair. And on the shoulder of her pinafore was a torn-out section which must fit the piece of material which Miss Rachel had taken from the keyhole.

Miss Rachel stumbled back out of the closet and fell against the wall. She felt sick from the stench of Mrs. Ruddick's blood. Most of all, she felt a desire to scream until the silence of the old house should fall apart like a tower of cards.

CHAPTER SIX

How SHE got out of the cellar, up the steps, and out upon the front porch, Miss Rachel was never to know. Her next coherent memory after the corpse of Mrs. Ruddick was the front walk, the gate, the subconscious idea of calling the police from the Byers house, so that the Hayeses would not have a hideous shock without warning.

She rang the bell at the Byerses', and it was answered promptly by Claudia's grandfather. By day he was small and lean, his skin brown and his white hair shining.

At his look of inquiry Miss Rachel stuttered: "Do you have a telephone? If you do—could I use it?"

"Of course." He opened the door and drew quickly backward. "It's here in the hall. There. At your left."

She had time to notice Bernice Byers, dust mop in hand, coming out of a door down the hall and Claudia looking at her over the banister of the stairs which went up at the right. Then she sat down at the little table which held the phone, dialed for Operator, and let the girl at the switchboard get the police for her. It was so much less nerve-racking than searching through a phone book.

She was holding her breath, waiting, when Bernice tapped her on the arm.

"Why are you calling the police?"

Miss Rachel didn't look up when she got out Mrs. Ruddick's name, but she sensed the change that came over Bernice Byers. The hand left her sleeve with a suggestion of distaste, and the dust mop made a little thud when it hit the floor.

"What's happened to Mrs. Ruddick?" Bernice asked after a moment.

But Miss Rachel was talking to the police. She was being somewhat incoherent, which made her angry at herself. She wished that she could have been one of those people who sit down quietly and say into the phone, "There's been a murder. Will you come out right away, please?" The desk sergeant wasn't being helpful. He didn't seem to want to believe her.

"Wait a minute," she said on sudden impulse. "Is Lieutenant Mayhew in?"

"Sure. Just came in," the phone crackled. "You want him to listen *too*, lady?"

Lieutenant Mayhew, lately transferred to the metropolitan district from his familiar bailiwick at Breakers Beach, might be a little annoyed at her bringing him another murder, but at least he understood things when he heard them. "Put him on, please," she asked.

Lieutenant Mayhew's big voice filled the phone comfortingly and then remained silent while Miss Rachel told him what she had in her closet.

When she had finished he said, "We'll be right out," and hung up.

Miss Rachel turned to face the Byerses, all four of them.

Ronald Byers had come out of what must be the dining room; there was a napkin balled in one hand. Bernice had put down the dust mop and backed away toward the stairs. Grandpa Byers stood by the door with one hand still clutching the knob. "There was among the three adults a mutual sick horror showing in their faces.

Claudia had reached the landing. She leaned over to look down at Miss Rachel in the hall. "Is Grandma Ruddick dead?"

Bernice jerked about. "Go to your room at once, Claudia." Claudia's unwilling feet took her up and out of sight.

Bernice bent a look on Miss Rachel in which anger had begun to grow. "I think that you might have prepared us for this. I should rather have had Claudia out of the way, and even we grownups would have appreciated a word in advance."

Miss Rachel thought back to her abrupt entry and crimsoned. "I'm very sorry. I was too upset to think."

"Nonsense," Ronald Byers put in. "Don't apologize. Who could have stopped to think after seeing what you must have seen? I'm glad that you came here instead of to the Hayeses'. It's going to be horrible for them."

Bernice made a sour mouth. "Why pity the Hayeses? It's going to be horrible for everybody."

Grandpa stirred away from the door. "Do you think it might have been suicide?"

"Not possibly," Miss Rachel said, trying not to remember why.

"And she was absolutely and completely dead?"

Under his gaze Miss Rachel could do no more than nod. Ronald Byers threw the napkin down upon a hall table and said, "Suppose you stay here, Miss Murdock, and let me go over and have a look around. We'll want to make sure that all the evidence is kept undisturbed until the police get there. I'll lock the place before I leave."

Bernice Byers stood tall and folded her arms. "Don't be a fool. Stay out of it until you're dragged in. You will be soon enough."

He walked past without looking at her. "Be back in a minute."

"Be careful," she shot after him.

Grandpa opened a door just beyond the telephone table. "You'll be more comfortable in here, miss. It's the living room." He glanced at Bernice. "We'd better wait together."

"I'll be down in a minute." Bernice turned and began running heavily upstairs. The Byers living room was furnished with an eye for show rather than quality. Miss Rachel wondered if Bernice had chosen the plush davenport in blue, the burgundy satin chair, the carpet in eggshell frieze. There was an air of striving for effect, as though the room were copied from a book or magazine with not quite the same grade of furnishings as the original. Done expensively, the room would have been striking, but it missed. It was self-conscious, regimented.

Miss Rachel sat on the blue davenport, and Grandpa Byers let himself down into the satin chair, and neither said anything until Ronald Byers reappeared in the hall.

Grandpa asked him, "Is it the way she says it was?"

Ronald was tight about the mouth, and sweat stood out on his face as though he had been running. "I didn't go into the cellar. I—I just checked through the other rooms." He brought a narrow article from behind him, wrapped in a single sheet of newspaper. He thrust it toward Miss Rachel, pulled the paper apart.

Miss Rachel almost fell off the davenport. Ronald Byers had brought home *the file!*

"But you shouldn't have moved it!" she cried when she could. "It's part of the evidence the police will want!"

The way he lowered his voice contained a warning she couldn't understand. "It was in your room."

"I know. I saw it there the first thing this morning."

He drew it away slightly. "You saw this file in your room?"

She was trying to understand. "Yes. Of course."

"It was—the way it is?"

He was getting whiter, and the hand holding the file shook a little, so that the paper rustled.

"It was just like that," she said. "And you didn't make any alarm?"

Suddenly his idea got over to her, his fear that the file being in her room was incriminating to her and his helpful hurry in bringing it out and his subsequent puzzlement that she hadn't started screaming at the first sight of it.

"My cat was gone too," she hastened to say, "and I thought the file had been used to kill it. You see—"

But there wasn't time to tell him about the toad or why the blood on the file had suggested the death of a pet cat. There was a police car coming up the street. It must by now be streaking between the empty lots of the abandoned subdivision, passing the little store at which Miss Rachel had bought her groceries.

Miss Rachel's thoughts had time to jump from the groceries to the paper bag to Mrs. Ruddick's blue bubbling-eye pin which should still be on the sink of the house next door before the police car stopped with a howl in the street outside.

Mayhew's brown, noncommittal face looked in at the doorway. He was still as big, as square, as brawny as Miss Rachel remembered him. When he came into the room and glanced at a chair Miss Rachel held her breath. Chairs should be specially reinforced for Mayhew. But his attention was attracted just then by the file in Ronald Byers' hands.

"This, I take it, is the weapon?"

There was no reproof for the removal of evidence in his tone or his look, but Miss Rachel was not fooled. Mayhew would find time to chide her for such sloppiness later. He took the file and examined it in its wrapping of newspaper. "Suppose," he said quietly to Ronald, "that you come back with me and show me just where you found this."

At the door Mayhew paused, glanced at Grandpa just behind him. "Will you ask everyone in the house to stay at home until they're interviewed?"

Grandpa nodded his understanding, and Mayhew and Ronald went out, Mayhew's figure shutting off the light like the enlarged bulk of a bear. Miss Rachel settled herself to be patient, but the next hour was a trying one. She knew what must be going on next door, with the elaborate machinery of crime detection in full swing, the ponderings of the coroner, the blaze of lights, the inch-by-inch examination of the whole house. She grew restless sitting on the davenport, and Grandpa came out of his abstraction long enough to go to the kitchen and bring her a drink.

Grandpa—she felt foolish using Claudia's name for him, but it somehow fitted—seemed oddly disposed to silence. Miss Rachel thought that she discerned a fear in him lest *she* start talking, a determination to keep staring at the wall lest he catch her eye and she open her mouth to say something.

Bernice came in with Claudia, and Grandpa repeated Mayhew's request that they remain at home. Bernice made no answer; she walked to the window that looked out toward Miss Rachel's house and stared through it. After a long while she said: "There's an ambulance coming. They're going to take her away."

Claudia wanted to get to the window, and Bernice turned on her savagely and drove her back. Claudia started to cry. "I want to see what it is. Is Grandma Ruddick really dead?"

"She's dead all right," Bernice said, "but you aren't going to see her. Quit crying. Here, dry your eyes."

Claudia sniffled into the offered handkerchief and looked from Miss Rachel to her grandfather. Miss Rachel did not feel free to offer the child any consolation in view of Bernice's severe attitude, and the grandfather seemed not to notice the tears.

Bernice stayed at the window, and at last she sighed. "They've taken her. She's gone." And a car drew off with a slow purr into the distance.

It was not long afterward that a uniformed man came and asked that they all come next door.

Bernice Byers flashed scorn at him. "And what about this child?"

"The child too, miss," he said imperturbably.

There was, Miss Rachel considered, something so old-maid auntish about Bernice that not even the policeman had been fooled into taking her for Claudia's mother.

When they walked into the stark living room of Miss Rachel's house and found the Hayeses and the Tellinghams already there, Mrs. Hayes in tears on the shabby davenport, Mr. Hayes giving her his shoulder, and the Tellinghams, with their maid, defiant in a row of chairs against the wall, Miss Rachel knew that somehow Mayhew had already begun to ferret out the relationship between these people.

More chairs were brought from the Hayeses' kitchen by two of Mayhew's men, and the group formed into a semicircle around three sides of the room. Mayhew took a chair, a straight-backed, thick-legged affair, and sat down on it gently. It shrieked. Mayhew stood up, remained standing the rest of the time.

He spoke first to the Hayeses. "You identify the body of the deceased as that of Mrs. Amanda Ruddick?"

Mrs. Hayes cried, "My mother!"

"Aged sixty-nine, a widow?"

Mr. Hayes answered doubtfully, "Well, the age is what she told us." And Mrs. Hayes covered quickly: "Of course. Mother always told the truth about everything."

Alma Tellingham's eyes, dark in a white face, swung to look at Mrs. Hayes. It was a long, deliberate glance. Alma's seersucker dress, severely made to fit her slenderness, was of dark blue. The color found an echo in her eyes, somehow heightened the effect of the look she gave Mrs. Hayes.

Mrs. Tellingham was aware of what Alma was doing. One hand twitched out toward the girl's and then stopped. She seemed to hold her breath.

As if sensing the girl's regard, Mrs. Hayes wiped her eyes and shot her a single spiteful glance. Alma seemed not to notice. She was staring through, not at, Mrs. Hayes, as though, Miss Rachel thought, she were looking beyond the woman at the statement she had just made, the fact of Mrs. Ruddick's truthfulness.

Mayhew said, "I'd like to know when you last saw the deceased."

"Last night when she went to bed," Mrs. Hayes replied. "She went to her room about nine o'clock. I asked if she wasn't going to fill her hot-water bottle, and she said she'd do it later."

"Was this usual?" Mayhew put in. Mrs. Hayes looked back blankly. "Did she usually wait to fill it?"

"Oh. No, she usually filled it in the bathroom and then went to her room with it and went to bed."

Mayhew seemed to think for a moment. "Then the fact that she didn't fill it when she went to her room at nine o'clock must have meant that she didn't plan on going immediately to bed."

"I suppose." Mrs. Hayes dabbed her eyes and looked at her husband. "What do you think, Bill?"

Mr. Hayes shrugged, wiped his eye with the back of his fist, wriggled the toe of a shoe. "I don't know. Could have meant anything, I guess. Maybe she'd decided all of a sudden that she didn't need it."

"No, she needed it." Mrs. Hayes blew her nose violently. "Poor Mother was so cold of nights. I think you're right, Lieutenant. She somehow didn't figure on going right to bed."

"Was the light in her room turned off?"

"We wouldn't know about that. Our room is upstairs, and hers was down and on the opposite side of the house."

"Did you hear any sound during the night that might have been your mother leaving the house?"

They shook their heads in unison, the big military-looking woman with the cold eyes and the little round man with a watery look of grief, and Mayhew swung from them to the Tellinghams.

In the instant before he spoke there was an obvious gesture of bracing herself on the part of Mrs. Tellingham. Her gray head came up a little; her mouth went tight. A trifle behind her, the maid sat with a Slavic expression of endurance. Alma made no move, but something flared in her eyes; fear, perhaps.

"You people are across the alley from where the deceased lived, and I note that your windows overlook the rear of these three houses. . . ."

Before he could finish Mrs. Tellingham said quickly: "We saw nothing. We were asleep."

Mayhew asked: "Did you hear anything?"

"Nothing at all." The pose of Mrs. Tellingham's head—high, nostrils out, eyes sharp with alarm—reminded Miss Rachel of a horse ready to plunge. The woman was alive with fear.

Mayhew seemed not to see but turned casually to Alma. "And you, Miss Tellingham?"

"I was asleep. I didn't hear or see anything."

Mayhew scribbled into his book, and Alma reached out a hand and took one of her mother's. The older woman relaxed so suddenly that her lips began shaking with the relief from strain. Ronald Byers had come into the room during the last few moments, and Mrs. Tellingham caught sight of him just inside the door. She forced her shaking lips to smile ever so little. Ronald answered with a nod.

Mayhew looked at the Slavic woman, half in shadow in the corner, and asked: "And what about you, Mrs. Karov?"

The Slavic mask opened its mouth and said, "I saw a light in the cellar here. It was a little light like a candle, moving about from window to window."

"When was this?" Mayhew asked.

"Last night."

"Do you know at about what time?"

She shook her head. If she felt the horrified stares of Alma and her mother, she gave no heed. "I don't know the time. It was very late."

"Did you see who was carrying the candle?"

"Mrs. Ruddick, I think."

There was a faint singsong accent in the way she spoke, a trace of deliberation in the speaking of each word. "Before she put out the candle there was someone came and watched through one of the windows. It was someone in a long coat." She paused and waited, and Miss Rachel saw the sudden strain in all of them—the Hayeses aghast, the Tellinghams unbelieving, Bernice and her father on guard, Ronald at the door like a man of stone.

"Who was this person?" Mayhew demanded. She said slowly, "It was the murderer—I think."

CHAPTER SEVEN

Mrs. Tellingham said with forced calm, "She's foreign, you know, and she's apt to jump to conclusions and exaggerate. . . ." Her voice died in the face of Mayhew's quick stare. "I thought perhaps she hadn't really—that she was making it up."

"Go on, Mrs. Karov."

The Slavic mask might have been hanging on the wall for all the human emotion it betrayed. "The person in the long coat went inside by the back door, and soon the light went out and everything was dark."

"Then what happened?"

She shook her head slowly. "Nothing more."

"You didn't see anyone leave the house?"

"I went back to bed. Why should I watch what goes on at night in this house of evil?"

"Why do you say that?" Mayhew snapped.

"It has sheltered a marriage without love and two deaths born of hatred," she intoned slowly.

"Shut up, Jessie," Ronald burst forth.

But under Mayhew's questioning she proceeded to tell of Ronald's marriage to Annie, of Annie's death and of Claudia's birth, and of the long estrangement between Alma and Ronald.

It seemed to Miss Rachel that Mrs. Karov got a curious feeling of importance out of being the first to let the police in on the ancient grievance among the three families.

Mayhew turned to the Hayeses: "What was Mrs. Ruddick's attitude concerning all this?"

Mrs. Hayes turned a look of hatred first on Alma Tellingham and then upon Ronald Byers. "My mother resented—we all resented—the treatment that Annie received in this house during the year she was married." And she went on to elaborate, and a scarlet flush spread over Alma's face, and Ronald turned dead white. "All these goings on," Mrs. Hayes concluded, "broke Annie's heart. She wasn't blind. It killed her, broke her heart in the end."

Mrs. Tellingham's high-pitched, nervous tone cut in: "Someone has to defend Alma in this. Why don't you tell the police that the marriage with Annie was a trap, a plot arranged to keep Ronald and Alma from realizing on the property her grandmother left them?"

Mrs. Hayes shut her mouth with a turtlelike snap. "If it was a plot I didn't hatch it. And Annie wouldn't have, poor darling."

"Why don't you tell them that Mrs. Ruddick planned it, lied and schemed and maneuvered and sacrificed her granddaughter to put it through?"

"What are you talking about?" Mayhew asked mildly.

Mrs. Tellingham was shaking again under the stress of anger and excitement. Her words tumbled over each other. "This all goes back some years, when my mother-in-law, Barbara Tellingham, was alive. At that time Ronald was engaged to Alma." Mayhew's eyes jerked to the persons she mentioned. Alma's head was forward; she seemed to be studying the floor. Ronald gave him back look for look, but not easily.

Mrs. Tellingham went on: "Mother was very ill, and she had no illusions about how much time was left her. She made a will, and since Alma and Ronald's marriage seemed only a matter of weeks, she left her property jointly to them. On their marriage, of course."

Something behind Mayhew's eyes had begun to gleam. "What about this property? What does it consist of?"

"The subdivision." When Mayhew's expression remained uncomprehending she gestured irritably toward the street. "All those empty lots you passed getting out here. Those were my mother-in-law's property."

Mayhew must have remembered the great weedy acreage, for he tried to keep disappointment out of his face. "And its present value?"

"We don't know," Mrs. Tellingham faltered. "You see, there hasn't been an offer for it for years, and now an airplane manufacturer wants it, and it may turn out to be quite valuable. But until the negotiations are finished . . ."

Mayhew revived at the fresh scent. He cut in: "And what disposition was finally made of this?"

Her mind went back slowly. "Well—under the terms of Mother's will . . ." She paused. "Perhaps I'd better explain first that Mrs. Ruddick and the elder Mr. Byers had been Mother's friends for years. She trusted their judgment and their business sense better than she did mine." Her eyes, on Grandpa, held resentment, an old anger for her mother-in-law's trust in him. "So that when her lawyer advised an alternate, on the rare chance that Alma and Ronald might not be married, she chose Mr. Byers and Mrs. Ruddick to act with me as a committee to administer the property."

"And they've done this?"

Mrs. Tellingham's hands clenched. "They've balked every effort I've made to get rid of it."

Mayhew walked to the window and back before putting his next question. "Was there any time limit to the marriage provision? I mean, suppose your daughter and young Mr. Byers should get married eventually in the future."

"They'd have the property in a minute," she snapped. And she was looking at Bernice Byers as if in defiance.

"This committee, then, was to function only until the marriage?"

"That's right."

He studied the lines of the decrepit radio with interest. "Has there been any attempt made to keep the marriage from taking place?"

She laughed bitterly, a short choked sound. "Doesn't it speak well for Mrs. Ruddick's plotting that for eight years my daughter and Mr. Byers haven't so much as spoken to each other?"

Mayhew walked to the radio and looked it over at close range. Miss Rachel has seen his tricks before, his care in keeping the center of interest off himself and what he was saying. When he (and Miss Rachel) was sure that everyone in the room had at least begun to notice the radio he said to Mrs. Hayes: "What happens to your mother's interest in this property?"

"Interest? She hasn't any interest, just a vote in controlling the sale. All that Mother had was the money she—" Mrs. Hayes paused, looked angrily at Mr. Hayes, as though he had caused her to say more than she had meant to.

"Go on," Mrs. Tellingham put in hotly. "Tell him about the money Mother left her."

"It wasn't much she was left with," Mrs. Hayes said just as hotly.

"How much was it?" Mayhew asked.

Her eyes dropped from his. "Three thousand."

Mayhew took a small account book from among the back leaves of his notebook. He walked to Mrs. Hayes, opened it, let her eyes probe it. "This was among the articles in your mother's room. Is it hers?"

Mrs. Hayes nodded with a touch of reluctance. "Yes, it was hers."

Mayhew inspected the entries. "It appears that your mother had in her account some twenty-one thousand dollars."

"She was a good businesswoman. She took the three thousand Barbara Tellingham left her and ran it up by shrewd investments."

"I see." Mayhew's glance drifted briefly to Grandpa. "Did Mr. Byers have a similar bequest?"

Grandpa spoke for himself. "No, no cash. There was to be a small salary paid for the management of the estate, but it's never been paid."

"The estate never earned it," Mrs. Tellingham snapped.

Mayhew tapped the account book. "Mrs. Hayes, did your mother leave a will disposing of this money?"

"I get it," she said flatly, as if daring Mayhew to suspect it as a motive for murder.

"And what of the estate, now that Mrs. Ruddick is dead?" He turned to Mrs. Tellingham. "Does this change the control in any way?"

She made a bitter mouth. "It gives me a fifty-fifty vote instead of a third." Her gaze slid over toward Grandpa. "There might be a possibility of liquidating the property—now."

It was a foolish remark in view of what the police were there to investigate, and Mrs. Tellingham must have known it. She turned a little pink, the color running thinly up into her sallow cheeks. "I mean," she stumbled, "there'll just be the two of us to manage things."

And that, somehow, sounded worse. Miss Rachel looked at Grandpa, in the corner between a watchful Claudia and a sneering Bernice, and she wondered if he caught the idea Mrs. Tellingham had unwittingly put over—that if the control of the Tellingham property were the motive for the murder, he or Alma's mother (or the both of them) had done the crime.

Grandpa Byers was looking preoccupiedly at the big figure of Mayhew. "For my part, if I legally could, I'd give you complete control," he said without glancing at Mrs. Tellingham. "It's been the anchor that's tied us here." And Miss Rachel recalled the overheard scrap of conversation in which Bernice and Grandpa had expressed their displeasure at the proximity of the Tellinghams, Alma in particular. "Barbara made it a last request, else I'd never taken part in the thing."

"You took part enough to lose the chance we had last year, the sale we might have made to the Mellix people."

He answered slowly, "If you had sold to them you wouldn't have the offer you have now from Airwasp." And Mrs. Tellingham, finding no answer, fell silent.

Mayhew chose the moment to switch back to the murder itself. Over the pretense of looking into his notebook he said abruptly: "Mrs. Ruddick was murdered in the basement closet at some time between midnight and two thirty or three. I'd like some sort of evidence to fix the time more closely than that estimated by the coroner's men." He raised his eyes and swept the group, and Miss Rachel remembered the story Claudia had told. Claudia, too, had seen the light in the basement, seen it extinguished.

When Miss Rachel began to speak she found that the attention of all the others had suddenly centered on her and, something more, a kind of enmity as against an interloper. "And you'd better ask Claudia to tell you," she finished, and found herself instantly in the background. Claudia had become the star.

Claudia told shyly about seeing the light, about thinking that it must be Miss Rachel, about the darkness of the intervening yard. No, she hadn't seen anyone in a long coat as Mrs. Karov had. The big street light at the corner had been out.

Mayhew sent a man to the telephone next door to ascertain at what time the street lights were turned off in this particular section, and he then proceeded to go back over Claudia's story inch by inch.

There was nothing more. There hadn't been any lights anywhere except the little candly one in the basement. She hadn't heard any doors opening, any sound of running, any human cry, though Mayhew's questions made all of them realize that Claudia at the window had been looking down innocently at the scene of her great-grandmother's brutal murder. She hadn't heard anything at all. But wait. She hadn't remembered before, but there had been a sound.

Miss Rachel's cat had been crying.

Samantha, half hidden behind the folds of Miss Rachel's skirt, took the limelight like a veteran. She yawned. She continued to look bored while Miss Rachel told of finding her in the pantry, lamed and covered with dust, obviously just emerged from the door of the cellar ajar behind her.

Mayhew looked respectfully at the yellow cat. "What do you think she'd be apt to do in a case such as what happened below?" Mayhew asked.

"She may have gone down, following Mrs. Ruddick, in the first place," Miss Rachel said thoughtfully. "If another person came on the scene and a struggle ensued I think she'd be frightened and start to mew."

"Perhaps we can reconstruct a bit of what happened." Mayhew said, He bent and touched Samantha's hind leg, and she flinched and struck out at him. "Mrs. Ruddick went to the basement with a candle to light her way. The cat followed. Someone came in and attacked Mrs. Ruddick, and the cat started to make a fuss, howling in fright, perhaps kept from getting out by the door being shut at the top of the stairs. With Mrs. Ruddick either dead or wounded too seriously to interfere, the murderer made for the cat with the idea of disposing also of it. The murderer either struck the cat hard enough to silence it or else couldn't quite kill it because it got out of his way."

Samantha looked beyond Lieutenant Mayhew at the circle of faces watching her, and then she howled, suddenly and dismally, as if at the memory of pain. Miss Rachel wondered what face, out of that circle, might have roused the cat, and Mayhew must have had much the same idea, for he bent and picked up the unwilling animal.

The yellow fur was bright between his hands; the green eyes stared in fury at his own.

Mayhew said, not quickly but casually, "Now, Mrs. Hayes, I want to know just why your mother came over here in the middle of the night and explored the cellar with a candle."

She tried to withdraw her attention from the cat, but she was still off guard when she said: "There were some letters she'd had, and she had some sort of idea they'd been hidden over here."

Mr. Hayes coughed in alarm.

Mrs. Hayes went on, "I don't know any more about it. Just

the letters. She might have been looking for them." Guard up, now. The military control very much in evidence. "She was always worrying over some trivial thing."

Mayhew put the cat down gently. "These letters—they were some that Mrs. Ruddick had received?"

In the minute that Mr. Hayes had coughed something about the group had changed. There was a new pattern of animosity, a new alignment of hatreds, as definite as a sudden switch of pawns in a game of chess. Miss Rachel put her mind to it, studied the faces of the people, and suddenly she saw it.

"They were letters which had come into my mother's possession," Mrs. Hayes was saying carefully.

"And how long had she had them?"

"I don't know. For years, I suppose. I'd never seen them. I couldn't identify them if you showed them to me."

"Do you know who wrote them or whom they were addressed to?"

She shook her head firmly, wiped her eyes with a gesture full of self-possession. "I haven't the slightest idea."

"Or what the contents might have been?"

This question startled her a little; she looked at Mayhew somewhat warily. "I didn't ever see them."

Miss Rachel took a leaf from Mr. Hayes's book; she coughed. Slightly at first, then hackingly. She sputtered a bit, too, to make it more authentic. Mayhew went on trying to pry something out of Mrs. Hayes about the letters and about Mrs. Ruddick's midnight prowls to find them, but most of the people in the room watched Miss Rachel in her spasm.

A detective put his head in and asked if he should bring her a drink.

Miss Rachel got up, choked out that she'd get it herself, and hurried out of the room. She hoped her departure in the middle of Mayhew's questions about the letters wouldn't be too obvious. If the box were there she meant to bring them back.

She went to the kitchen, made a pretense of drinking at the sink, then slipped to the pantry and approached the cellar door.

There were men in the cellar; their voices drifted up to her. An occasional clanking sound connected somehow in her mind with the furnace.

She stepped in upon the stairs and peeped over. Below, and to the rear, two men were sifting the ancient ashes from the furnace, working slowly and methodically, their attention upon what they were doing. Miss Rachel went soundlessly down to the loose step, reached for the piece of planking that covered the hole containing the box. It came out with a slight rasp, and she put her hand in.

The box was there, the metal cold to her touch. She drew it out without noise, replaced the plank, and hurried back into the pantry. And there she found Mayhew waiting for her.

He put out a big hand without saying anything, and Miss Rachel meekly put the box into it and watched his face as he raised the lid. He'll be pleased, she thought, when he finds the letters. But Mayhew's face remained a blank.

Slowly he let the box revolve until she could see into it. And there was nothing there.

CHAPTER EIGHT

MISS RACHEL told him what she could. "The letters were from Alma, addressed to Ronald Byers. In the one I started to read she was telling him her grief and remorse over their treatment of Annie."

"And Annie was dead?"

"From what was in the letter, I thought so."

"Then repentance was a little late, wasn't it?"

Miss Rachel looked beyond Mayhew's frown, trying to fit the parts of the puzzle. "You see, Ronald hadn't meant to marry Annie—not really. There must have been some sort of trick to it, some scheming on Mrs. Ruddick's part."

"You believe what Mrs. Tellingham says about it?"

"Somehow—yes. I think that after the marriage, which Mrs. Ruddick must have brought about in order to have a share in controlling the Tellingham property, that Ronald and Alma, in their frustration, took out their spite on Annie. She was, of course, the person who stood between them, even though she had been the tool of Mrs. Ruddick. And yet she hardly deserved that year of misery. That's what must have tortured Alma and Ronald after Annie's death—the memory of their treatment of her, her helplessness in the face of it."

Mayhew stared into the empty box. "And these letters?"

"They would have shown Ronald Byers that Alma had a heart."

"I see. They could have been stolen by Mrs. Ruddick to prevent Ronald from thinking that Alma *was* sorry, to lead him to believe that she was a cold-hearted devil who had no regrets about Annie."

"And being in the depths of remorse himself, he might easily have blamed Alma for all of it, decided in some twisted way that she had caused him to abuse Annie. You know how men are."

Mayhew shot her a shrewd glance. "You women will never quite forgive Adam, will you? But I see your point. Stealing the letters might keep Alma and Ronald apart, just as the marriage had. We'd better pin Mrs. Hayes down on exactly how long her mother had had these letters."

She looked toward the door. "Are the others still in there?"

"I let them go with a suggestion they have breakfast. I'm advising you to do the same. If you try to keep going on an empty stomach you won't do so well."

"I couldn't eat in here." She made a shuddery gesture of distaste.

"Get your wrap and let me drive you to a café." He took her arm gently and urged her out of the closet. "The thing I'm most interested in now," he went on dryly, "is just how *you* got into all this."

Miss Rachel watched butter disappear into the square holes of a waffle and thought that she'd never be able to eat it, but she did. And talked as well, telling Mayhew the initial part of her adventure: the queer sense of alarm she'd had over the dead toad, the watching Slavic woman, the signs of occupancy in an empty room above, and her first meetings with Ronald Byers and Mrs. Ruddick.

Mayhew took it all in along with an omelet and a piece of ham. His square brown face reflected no feeling except a mild thoughtfulness. But over the second cup of coffee he said, "Then at the time you came on the scene we can presume that two important things were about to happen. Ronald Byers must have been about ready to resume openly his love affair with Alma Tellingham. They'd been meeting secretly in the upstairs room, but there was really no longer any barrier to their romance once the misunderstanding about the letters was explained. Secondly, there was to be an offer made for the property Barbara Tellingham had left in her involved and foolish will. Now, both these things concerned Mrs. Ruddick."

"I'd meant to tell you," Miss Rachel said, remembering. "When the conversation switched from the property to the hidden letters I sensed a change in the group of people. It took me a moment to realize what it was. You see, it's that all of those people—Bernice and the elder Mr. Byers, Alma and Ronald and Mrs. Tellingham—all of them had reason to kill Mrs. Ruddick, but for utterly different reasons. The discussion about the property brought out one set of hatreds in the group; the tricks Mrs. Ruddick had used to keep Alma and Ronald apart brought out another. It's like two patterns in a rug, overlapping each other."

"It's a double plot in a tragedy of errors," Mayhew said dourly. "Mrs. Ruddick had involved herself in two sets of circumstances, either of which could have been the motive for her murder. As I said before, at the time you butted in on things affairs were coming more or less to a climax. Ronald and Alma, at long last and in spite of her scheming, were very apt to be married.

"An offer was to be made for the subdivision which couldn't logically be turned down. In either case the estate would pass out of Mrs. Ruddick's hands entirely. I think that prospect would hurt the sense of importance which a person of her type has to an astonishing degree." He stared into his cup. "Perhaps she was trying to do something to prevent one or both of these things from happening." After a long moment he said, "There has to be a motive somewhere."

Miss Rachel felt a little chill run up her back. She was remembering her first glimpse of Mrs. Ruddick, on the porch with her dyed hair like a yellow halo above her wrinkled face. There hadn't been much sign, outwardly, of Mrs. Ruddick's liking to play God in other people's lives. There had been no indication of omnipotence in her waddling walk, her simpering ways. She'd been rather simple-looking, really, even when she had forced Miss Rachel to listen to her extended account of the family quarrel lest her sympathies stray in the wrong direction. And when she had been caught trespassing she'd been actually apologetic. The excuse about hunting for the brooch had been thin, of course. . . .

Miss Rachel choked on a piece of waffle, picked up her purse and got out of her chair, and started for the door.

"What's come over you?" Mayhew demanded, catching up.

Miss Rachel nearly fell over herself getting into the police car. "The brooch," she panted. "Oh, how stupid of me! I let it lie there!"

Mayhew tried not to hurry or look puzzled. "Mind explaining?"

Above the clash of gears Miss Rachel got out: "Mrs. Ruddick wore a pin, a blue-eye sort of thing with a frame of pearls. She left it in my house as an excuse to come back and prowl.

I've no doubt that if I'd gotten up in the middle of last night and caught her in the cellar she'd have said she was looking for her pin."

"And what about it now?"

"It wasn't on her in the closet, but while I was down there investigating someone slipped into my kitchen and left it on the sink."

His eyes jerked from the road to give her a sharp glance. "And you think you know who it was?"

"No." She watched telephone poles slip past, the first lots of the empty subdivision come into view across a hill. "But there must be some clue in the fact that it was left there—that it was important enough to risk being seen to replace it."

"Perhaps the murderer thought it valuable and stole it."

"No one would ever take it for anything but a ten-cent-store trinket."

"Perhaps he didn't know he had taken it." Mayhew frowned into the sun that gilded the tall grass of the lots as they slid past. "A pin such as you describe could easily have caught on his clothes during the struggle Mrs. Ruddick put up. He may have inspected his clothes or disposed of them early this morning and found it."

"What about clothing? Wouldn't there be some trace—?"

"If there is a trace we'll find it. I've put in for search warrants for all the houses at the end of the street. But something tells me we're a little too late."

He put on the brakes, and the car slowed to a stop at Miss Rachel's gate. She had time to see a face—Mr. Hayes's, she thought—disappear quickly from a window next door and to hear Bernice Byers call Claudia irritably to come inside and to stay there. Then she was into her hall, seeing a detective get up in surprise from the chair he had placed at the foot of the stairs and hurrying toward the kitchen.

For a moment she experienced a quick, inexplicable fear, but the brooch was there, pushed back upon the sink board, just as Miss Rachel remembered it as being. Only the fact that the detectives had not known that it belonged to the dead woman had kept it from being collected as evidence.

Mayhew picked it up between two handkerchief-wrapped fingers and held it toward the light. The blue stone winked and glittered; the bubbly pearls were like a little rim of tears. Mayhew turned the pin over and inspected the catch. Here was evidence that his theory would hold water—the hooked section which should have held the hasp was pulled far over, out of line. Warking gingerly, Mayhew tried to close the lock, but it would no longer meet.

"This damage must have been done since she wore it; she couldn't have kept it on in this shape." He turned the pin again, and Miss Rachel noticed what she had failed to see before, that one of the numerous pearls was missing.

She pointed the damage out to him.

"Dropped and stepped on in the fight," he said cryptically. "Must have fastened to the murderer's clothes in some inconspicuous place and been carried away without being noticed. Taking the risk of returning it here, especially after putting you on your guard with the bloody file, must have been the first reaction of terror." He weighed the pin, letting the light settle on the facets of the stone.

"It could as well have been thrown into a trash barrel and discovered there."

The last sentence gave Miss Rachel a clue to how thoroughly the detectives, who formerly had swarmed in this house, were by now scattered among the other three and going through things with a fine comb.

Mayhew put the pin, still in the handkerchief, carefully into his pocket. He looked gratified and alert, like a good hunting dog who begins to smell the game. He went to the cellar stairs and looked down.

"Suppose you come down with me and do a little acting."

Miss Rachel followed obediently, and during the next hour she demonstrated her initial exploration of the cellar, her finding of Mrs. Ruddick's body, her accidental discovery of the box containing the letters. In addition, in other parts of the house Mayhew satisfied his curiosity concerning just how the file was placed when she first saw it that morning and whether there were any other entrances or exits to the house save the front or back doors. There was a bare possibility that a window could have been forced if necessary, but it would have been a noisy and awkward process.

"Mrs. Ruddick must have had a key to the place," Mayhew said, examining the last of the downstairs windows.

"And Ronald Byers must have too," Miss Rachel answered.

"We'll check that." Mayhew tested the window latch, found it firm. "I'm going to examine all keys I can lay my hands on. Any that fit these locks will be appropriated."

"Speaking of Ronald Byers," Miss Rachel said, her brow wrinkling, "I told you at breakfast about my first meeting with him. I'm sure he had come here to meet Alma and that when I went upstairs and let a little light shine from under his black-out arrangement at the window, that it was Alma who started to come in at the kitchen. What I'm wondering is whether you found the black cloth and the candle he kept up there."

"We haven't found them, but he hasn't had time, either, to dispose of them."

"When he was so anxious to come over alone after I told them of the crime I'm pretty certain it was to remove all traces of his and Alma's rendezvous before the police came and asked questions."

Mayhew nodded, but Miss Rachel had a feeling that he was now ready to get rid of her. She had given him a background for the crime, described the personality of the dead woman, clarified Mrs. Ruddick's relations with the people about her, laid down the woof and the warp of the thing for him to embroider. And now—she sensed it clearly—he was eager to get her away where she would be safe and where she wouldn't get into any further mischief.

The situation was a familiar one to Miss Rachel, for Lieutenant Mayhew had appropriated murder from her before, but she nevertheless resented it fiercely. She had a sudden mental picture of where he now wished her to be, safely and stodgily at home, getting news of the official progress via the newspapers while Mayhew himself went through all sorts of excitement finding the culprit. The hair along her small aged neck moved in anger, a bristling sensation.

She and Mayhew would have, at this point, begun arguing, except that a detective ran up the rear steps and into the kitchen and laid down upon the sink a hasty-looking bundle made up of a black cloth, a box of thumbtacks, and a candle.

"Found this stuff in a drainpipe which goes down on the side next the Byers place," the detective said briefly.

Mayhew let it lie. "I know what it is. Tell Ronald Byers I want to see him, will you?"

The detective left, and Mayhew turned to Miss Rachel with

an expression of cordial hurry. "Miss Murdock, I suggest you go home. I don't like to be abrupt, but since a crime has been committed here and the house seems to have been the center of a good deal of plotting and hatred, I think you'd be safer there. Suppose you run along and call me later. I'll let you in on anything new.

She had him at a disadvantage, of course, because they were old friends, and Mayhew's wife will never forget that it was Miss Rachel who brought them together. She stood thoughtful in the middle of the kitchen, and the light from the window over the sink made her white hair shine and her skin glow with the soft patina of well-cared-for silk. The look she turned on Mayhew, though, was wary.

"Can you make me go?" she asked.

He stifled something he wanted to say. "No, I can't legally force you to leave." He waited, a patient moment. "I'm asking you to. Just to do me a favor."

He was being so awfully nice about it that Miss Rachel almost weakened. He looked big and brown and capable and kind, and Miss Rachel had a sudden insight into how much Sara must love him. It was this thought of Sara that decided her. Really, for his own good, someone ought to be here, someone with intuition, that is. It had always amazed Miss Rachel how little intuition Mayhew actually had. Things could go on right under his nose—that enmity between Mrs. Tellingham and Mrs. Hayes, for instance.

She shook her head firmly. "I'm sorry. I'm not going because you need me."

For an instant he looked incredulous. "We need you? But, forgive me for saying it, you're—you're—"

Miss Rachel cut in smoothly, "I'm seventy. I haven't the

strength of a mouse. I'm a woman. That's what you mean, don't you? Well, stop and think a moment. I was here long enough to size up all these people before a murder put them on their guard. I met and talked at length with the dead woman. And I have imagination."

He tried to oblige, to consider what she had said, but his impatience burst forth. "Still, I'm going to ask you to go."

She shook her head again.

"If I felt that the crime were the end of what's been going on here I wouldn't ask you," he went on, "but there are several loose ends I don't like. First, if Mrs. Ruddick were searching for the letters and found them, where are they now? Secondly, if the control of the Tellingham property were the motive for the murder, there still remain two people, each having an equal vote, to carry on the feud. Then, of course, you've got that odd angle about the meanness to the little girl. Not to mention a murderer whose idea of a joke seems to have been to leave the blood-and-brain-smeared weapon he'd used on Mrs. Ruddick in your room for you to see first thing in the morning."

"He's insane," Miss Rachel decided, trying to dust off her intuition in a hurry.

"He's trying to frighten you enough to get rid of you," Mayhew told her. "The bloody file was a warning, a brutal and emphatic one. Returning the pin this morning might have been an idea along the same line, something to puzzle and frighten you and force you to leave." His tone coaxed her. "Take my advice and go home."

Miss Rachel entertained a mental picture of boredom and anxiety. She smoothed her collar, adjusted her cuffs. "I want to be in on things. And besides that"—she paused for emphasis—"it's my house, you know. I've rented it for a month."

He sighed, turned to the window. "I'll talk with you later. I see my man bringing Ronald Byers. Suppose you wait in your room while I talk with him."

She went off with a feeling of having won the first round. In the front hallway she admitted a young man who introduced himself as a member of the press and took her picture. Heretofore the reporters had paid attention only to Mayhew. The young man's interest added to her feeling of victory. When the reporter had gone she went upstairs and gave intuition a fling by looking into all the bedrooms. In the room that Ronald had used she walked to the window and looked out. The yard below was sunny. It must be near to noon. The tangle of roses looked warm, hushed, drowsy.

All the parts of a familiar pattern then rushed into place. Claudia got out of her swing and walked through the little gate into Miss Rachel's yard; the Slavic maid came out and stood immobile, watching. And with a snip-snip-snip Mr. Hayes came into sight, engaged in his everlasting job of cutting his hedge.

A sudden, not easily explained, fear contracted Miss Rachel's heart. The garden was still—too still. And Claudia was so little.

There had been two patterns touching Mrs. Ruddick, and Mrs. Ruddick was dead. Miss Rachel clutched the window frame and kept her eyes on Claudia. The child moved aimlessly among the rosebushes toward the white stone that marked the grave of the toad.

Which pattern made of Mrs. Ruddick's scheming also involved and endangered Claudia?

CHAPTER NINE

MISS RACHEL woke and looked into an encircling darkness so intense that for a moment she was frightened, forgetting where she was. She sat up quickly, feeling the bedclothes fall away. There was no movement of air, no scrap of sound. She put out a hand to feel of something that pressed her foot through the layer of blankets and encountered Samantha's furry warmth. The cat purred under her touch, gave forth a sleepy meow.

Miss Rachel's eyes were growing used to the dark. She could make out the shine of the dressing-table mirror, the black rectangle of the closet door, the pale square of the window. And she knew, too, where she was. She was still in the house on Beecher Street.

She recalled the day just past from the moment when she awoke to see the bloody file leaning against the wall to the time when Mayhew had gone reluctantly away with a warning to take care of herself. His offer of a man to sleep in the house she had refused because acceptance would have looked like an admission of fear and would have been a further lever in Mayhew's effort to get her out. It had been a long day, a worrisome and frightening day.

In an attempt to distract Claudia from the general morbidity she had had the child help her in transplanting a fuchsia. Mr. Hayes had made offer of the plant, peering across from the other side of the hedge when Miss Rachel and Claudia met in the garden. She had drawn out the slight task, made great ceremony of choosing the right spot, getting the hole dug just so, putting in leafmold and sand and borrowed manure, also supplied by Mr. Hayes.

They had put the fuchsia very near the burial place of the toad. Claudia had plucked off one pale purplish blossom and laid it beside his headstone. She had looked grave and depressed, but the dead pet had apparently roused in her no thought of the fate of her great-grandmother. She had, during the hour or more she spent with Miss Rachel, mentioned Mrs. Ruddick but once, and that only in connection with the brooch. She had asked Miss Rachel if anyone had found her grandmother's pin, and when Miss Rachel said that they had it seemingly satisfied her.

Claudia had gone home at about one, and the rest of the day had passed in an atmosphere of suspense. Mayhew, she knew, was talking things over in detail with the others. There was a mass turning out of trash barrels and garbage pails by his subordinates—undoubtedly in search for any clothing which had had to be discarded by the murderer because of bloodstains. So far as Miss Rachel could discover by careful watching no important discoveries were made.

She had eaten a small cold dinner in the living room, the kitchen still having somehow a too-close association with the cellar, and after a good-night lecture from Mayhew in which he carefully told her nothing of the afternoon's developments she had come to bed.

And now here she was, wide awake in the middle of the night; and worse, she was hungry.

She thought of the length of hallway and stair to be traversed on her way to the kitchen. There wasn't anything good down there, either, except bread and butter and tea. And the can of tuna.

"One just doesn't eat tuna in the middle of the night," she thought firmly, trying to put it out of her mind. But the tuna came back mixed with lettuce and rich with mayonnaise, made into a sandwich between two slices of fresh bread.

She lay back and curled deep in the covers and tried to go to sleep. Beyond the pane the sky was beginning to look a trifle gray. How foolish to want to get up and eat the tuna when breakfast couldn't be far off! She shut her eyes determinedly, breathed deeply in an imitation of slumber. But the tuna stayed in her mind's eye, richly delicious between the soft white bread.

In the end she got out of bed and put on a robe and slippers, switched on the lights in her room and in the hall, and went down to eat. By the time she reached the kitchen the house, from out of doors, must have presented an appearance of festivity. There were lights everywhere. Miss Rachel ate her sandwich and drank her tea in a blaze of glory.

She had shut the door to the pantry; she put the cellar out of her thoughts. When the tuna was gone she sat for a while sipping the last of the tea. It must have been almost an hour since she had first wakened before she stirred, put her dishes in the sink, turned out the kitchen light, tested the back-door latch, and went out into the front hall.

She was just beside the front door, her finger on the switch, when a feeling of sudden nervousness took possession of her. There had been some sort of sound, undefinable, minute, connected somehow with the wall by which she stood. She listened, ears straining and breath stopped, for its repetition. Old houses creaked and groaned sometimes of their own accord; she knew this from living in her own house, built for fifty years. The sound she had heard might have been innocent, accidental.

When she had waited for some seconds and heard nothing more she pressed the switch and went upstairs. Her shadow followed, long and black, to the upper hall, where she pressed another switch and went on into her room. Here everything was as she had left it, the bed neatly turned down and the cat at its foot.

The cat was looking at the window.

The pane was raised less than a foot; the tattered shade came a trifle below the center division. The glass was black, and the room was reflected in it. Outside, so far as Miss Rachel could see, there was nothing. She stroked the cat and coaxed it to lie down. Then she took off her robe and slippers, put out the light, and went to her bed. She sat on the edge and pressed the center springs until they squeaked. Then she got up without any sound and went to the window.

The night was not entirely dark. From far off came the glow of metropolitan Los Angeles, subdued now because the hour was late, but still bright enough for Miss Rachel to see the sloping porch of the roof and the figure that was crouched there.

Her heart gave a terrible lurch as she first caught sight of the column of blackness which gradually identified itself as a human form. A scream rose in her throat, tearing its way to her lips, and then she saw the thing moving. Moving away. Without sound, without any awkwardness; and she watched, half expecting it to float off into the air in the same uncanny and effortless way that it was approaching the roof edge.

It made for a certain spot and stood there. Miss Rachel strained her eyes in an attempt to see what was happening.

There seemed to be a slow foreshortening taking place, a downward absorption into the shingles. Miss Rachel's thought leaped from the possibility of utter magic to a more practical trap door, and then she remembered the sturdy latticework which closed in one side of the porch. Of course—it would be a natural ladder.

A kind of impatient anger chased away her fear. Here was a prowler getting away without being identified. She forgot her terror when the prowler's destination had been uncertain. She wanted only to see the face that belonged to that dark silent form.

She ran to the light switch and turned it on and ran back to the window, unhooked the screen and pushed it out and raised the pane far enough to lean through. The light cast her silhouette on the shingles, made enough illumination for her to see the edge of the roof. There was nothing there, but the dry tendrils of a vine which had once covered the trellis were shaking violently. Then the trellis itself began to rattle and groan. Evidently the light from above had been seen by the intruder; he was intent now upon getting away, noise or no noise.

Miss Rachel ran into the hall and down the steps to the front door, where she paused long enough to throw the switches for both the front hallway and the porch. Then she drew the night latch open and almost fell over herself getting out.

The two globes in the porch ceiling made bright the entire front of the house, so bright that Miss Rachel could see the dry leaves on the trellis still shaking, a few of them spiraling slowly to the floor. But there was no person on the trellis. In the time it had taken her to run downstairs he had escaped.

She went to the corner by the trellis and looked off into the dark. This was the space of yard between her house and the Byerses', and while she watched nothing moved in it.

She stepped back with an odd feeling of cold, realizing now that she was outside in nothing but a gown. It had been a foolish and dangerous act to have tried to identify the prowler. Mayhew would have been angry if he had known. Her eyes roved over the trellis in a last desultory glance. She had better go in.

For a moment she failed to take in the small object that hung among the dried bits of vine. It was dark blue and inconspicuous, wedged solidly between an upright and a crossbar, a little above the level of her eyes. With a cautious finger she pried it free.

It was a button, perhaps an inch and a half in diameter, of smooth plastic with a raised oak-leaf design in its center and a milled border. Attached was a collection of black thread. Miss Rachel shut it quickly into her hand. The prowler had lost it in his hurry, and now it was hers.

She went back into the house, but she spent no more time in bed. When dawn came it found her fully dressed in the living room, listening to an all-night record program on the radio.

Mayhew came out early and commented on the fact that she looked sleepy.

Still looking sleepy, she proceeded to tell him of her early-morning adventure and took satisfaction from the way it electrified the lieutenant. The button she kept to herself, not without qualms of conscience, but with a determination to have a bit of inside track over Mayhew. She omitted telling him of it. After all, Mayhew had all the resources of the police, and she had—only a button. She hugged the knowledge of its presence, sewn securely on the inside border of her petticoat.

Mayhew then plodded on into a subject that was becoming familiar. "Your sister is very much frightened for your safety. She called me last night, asked for some way in which she could talk to you without coming out here. She's afraid of this place." His glance implied that if Miss Rachel were a normal little old lady she'd feel likewise. "The newspaper stories were pretty gruesome. Don't you think you owe it to your sister's peace of mind to go home to her?"

"I'll call her on the telephone," Miss Rachel promised glibly without answering his question.

"This incident last night." He paused to lend weight to his words. "It might have ended much differently."

"I might have caught him," she considered brightly.

"I'm afraid that if you had seen his face you wouldn't have lived to tell about it." He leaned toward Miss Rachel from the opposite side of the radio. "Please. Go home."

The radio announcer cut off the music to read a commercial about canned ham. "I'm hungry," Miss Rachel decided. "I believe I'll have breakfast. Would you join me in a cup of coffee?"

He shook his head. "I'll see you later." He retrieved his hat and made for the front door.

When Miss Rachel saw him making a detailed examination of the trellis she felt a bit sorry for him, almost inclined to turn over the button as an act of good will. She controlled the impulse by recalling his efforts to shut her out of things.

Later, in the kitchen at breakfast, she was surprised to have him go through on his way to the cellar. While she nibbled toast and sipped coffee she kept an ear cocked for the vague sounds he made below. He was hunting for something. The men who had been sifting the ashes had been hunting for something. What was it he had told her was missing? Her mind rummaged through their former conversations. The letters, of course. The letters Mrs. Ruddick had stolen to keep Ronald from knowing Alma's feelings, the letters that had been stolen from Mrs. Ruddick and for which she continued to search, the letters Miss Rachel had stumbled upon when she had first gone down into the cellar.

Mayhew must think that they were still down there. Perhaps the story of her night's adventure had given him the idea that the intruder had wanted them. Exactly what, Miss Rachel wondered, was the point in their possession? Was it that so long as they weren't found there would be a doubt in Ronald Byers' mind about Alma—a doubt carefully nurtured by the murderer to keep them apart? Or had Ronald himself killed the old woman in uncontrollable rage at her meddling in his life and now sought the letters as a form of self-justification for what he had done?

She moved her ankle, felt the nubby hardness of the button on the inside of her petticoat. She was breaking the law, of course.

This line of uneasy thought was broken by the sound of movement outside the kitchen door. A shadow focused itself on the pane. Miss Rachel stood up. There was a soft rapping on the wooden section, a sly turning of the knob.

Miss Rachel looked through the glass to see the Slavic woman, her nose flat on the outer screen, trying to stare into the room. When she unlatched and opened the door the woman stepped back as if uncertain of her welcome. The high cheekbones were shiny, the eyes defensive.

"Hel-lo," she said in the slow singsong Miss Rachel had heard the previous morning. "You all alone in here?"

Miss Rachel tried to make herself taller, to keep the Slavic woman from examining the room across her shoulders. "Hello," she said briskly. And as the woman continued to peer nervously: "Are you looking for someone?"

Mrs. Karov shook her head. "No. Not looking for anybody. Could I come in. Please?" She put out a big foot as if to advance.

"The police are here," Miss Rachel admonished.

The foot drew back; something veiled came into the narrow eyes. "They still here?"

Lieutenant Mayhew at that moment came into the room from the cellar. He stopped when he saw Mrs. Karov. "Were you looking for somebody?" he asked, almost duplicating Miss Rachel's question.

For an instant Miss Rachel thought that the woman was about to sneeze; then she saw that the grimace was intended for a smile. One of Mrs. Karov's hands came out from behind her, and in it was a small glass container. It came in Miss Rachel's direction, paused, and was displayed. It was a glass of jelly.

"You like jelly? This is boysenberry. It's good. Made yesterday." Miss Rachel felt the glass slide into her hand.

Mrs. Karov began to withdraw shyly, hands smoothing her apron, her eyes flitting from Mayhew's face to the jelly she had given Miss Rachel. "Tell me if you like it," she said finally just before she turned and walked rapidly away.

Mayhew snatched the jelly out of Miss Rachel's hand and held it to the light.

It was transparent, a lovely red, innocent under its thin lid of paraffin. "Don't eat it," he decided, putting it on the table.

Miss Rachel looked at it with interest. "Do you suppose it's poisoned?" she wondered. "Wouldn't that be terribly risky, giving out poisoned stuff in daylight like that?"

He drummed on the table with the tips of his fingers. He seemed to have already forgotten the jelly, forgotten Mrs. Karov.

"What did you find in the cellar?" Miss Rachel asked after a considerable period of silence.

He came back from some far mental exploration, looked at Miss Rachel as though he had only half caught what she had said.

"As long as you're determined to stay here," he said gruffly, "I want you to promise me one thing."

"Yes?

His fingers stopped drumming and clenched into a fist. He looked as if he wanted to pound the table. "I want you to promise me that you won't, under any circumstances, go down into the cellar again."

"Oh, of course not," Miss Rachel said demurely.

Mayhew took it as agreement, since he was really thinking about something else anyway, but in Miss Rachel's mind the conversation stood this way:

Mayhew: I want you to promise me . . .

Herself: Oh, of course not. (I couldn't promise *that*!)

So when Mayhew went away in the direction of the Hayes-es', Miss Rachel lost no time in getting down into the cellar. She was tired of Mayhew's being so closemouthed, and, besides, she might be able to find the thing that everyone else had missed.

CHAPTER TEN

Mrs. Hayes opened the door to Mayhew and let him see that she resented and disliked him before she said, "Yes? What can I do for you?"

Mayhew said, "I'd like to talk to you for a moment about your mother."

"Again?" She put on a sour expression of weariness. "Well, come in."

The house was well furnished and decorated in good modern style, belying its old-fashioned exterior. Mayhew sat down in a red wing chair, and Mrs. Hayes took a stiff pose on a sofa opposite.

He let a moment go by in getting out his notebook and pencil. Mrs. Hayes stared in military scorn. "These letters your mother had had," he said finally. "I want you to tell me when you first remember knowing that she had them."

Her large bosom swelled with a long breath. "I've said before, I know very little about them. I had always thought it was some childish prank, some saving of old letters which someone had thrown away. You know how old people are."

"This was something quite different," Mayhew said smoothly. "It happens that these letters were addressed to Ronald Byers by Alma Tellingham. He never received them, did not know of their existence until recently. The obvious conclusion is that your mother took them before they reached him."

Mrs. Hayes bristled. "I wouldn't know anything about that."

"This is a police inquiry," Mayhew reminded her. "And your mother is dead. We can't hurt her now by telling the truth about her faults, and we can get at the truth and perhaps discover her murderer."

Mrs. Hayes looked at him fixedly. "Ronald Byers is very vengeful," she said, putting into words the thought Mayhew had meant her to have. "He might have killed her. If he did I hope he hangs."

"About the letters," Mayhew prompted.

She circumvented any implication of guilt for herself. "I didn't know at the time, of course. When I did find out what had happened it was so long after that I figured it wouldn't do any good to try to straighten things out. You see, Mother stayed with Annie constantly at the end, and for about a month afterward she kept on at the house, taking care of the baby and packing Annie's things away. It must have been during that month that she got hold of the letters. Ronald was at work during the day; he wouldn't have known about them. He and Alma had had the decency to terminate their disgraceful affair, so the woman couldn't have asked if he'd gotten them."

"And how long was it before you knew that Mrs. Ruddick had them?"

"Several years. By then, of course, Ronald and Claudia had moved back with his people, and the affair with Alma was as dead as a doornail."

"Didn't it occur to you that the reason it *was* dead was because these letters hadn't been delivered?"

She shrugged her big shoulders. "I'm sorry. It wouldn't have changed things any if I had known. You've got to remember that Annie was my daughter and that Alma had made her last year of life miserable by carrying on with Annie's husband."

Mayhew waited a moment before he said, "About your daughter's marriage. Do you mind telling me just what happened, how it was that he married your girl after being engaged to Miss Tellingham?"

Some of the military firmness went out of her body; there was a suggestion of droop. "I don't really know. I was surprised, really, when it happened. Annie was so young—too young."

"Ronald Byers says that he got an anonymous telephone call that Alma was meeting a man, a former sweetheart, downtown. He got in his car and drove past the corner where the rendezvous was supposed to be kept, and Alma was standing there. He parked the car and walked back. He accused her of waiting for her former lover, and she resented it. Their tempers flared up and they had a hot quarrel. He believed what he had heard from his anonymous tip in the way that people are prone to believe most in what they fear. In revenge, he began going with Annie, who seemed mysteriously available every time he started anywhere."

Mrs. Hayes had quit looking at him. She was staring at her lap where her fingers were twisted together in a harsh grip.

"Things drifted along," Mayhew continued, "and he grew fond of Annie and more and more convinced that Alma no longer loved him. He and Annie were married one forenoon on the spur of the moment. I suppose it took some time for him to realize his mistake, to begin to wonder about the telephone call, to see Alma and straighten things out. In that first conversation they decided that Mrs. Ruddick was at the bottom of things, that she had been the voice on the anonymous phone call, that she had pushed Annie out as a pawn to attract Ronald. Her motive was obvious. If Ronald and Alma had married there would have been no committee to administer the Tellingham estate. As things were, Mrs. Ruddick was in a position of considerable importance. And she liked that."

Still Mrs. Hayes said nothing, made no move.

"Ronald and Alma proceeded to carry on as though the marriage to Annie didn't exist. I can understand your daughter's feelings. It was a cruel, thoughtless way to get even, but fate proceeded to catch up with them when Annie died. There must have been instant regret, harsh self-condemnation. Ronald says that he went through a hell he didn't know existed, that even today he would give the rest of his life if he could only relive that year and be decent to his bride. Well, he couldn't. And for a while, of course, he and Alma had no desire to see each other. She wrote to tell him how she felt. If he could have known that she shared that hell of self-loathing in which he lived they would have been drawn together. Eventually, when time had worn away the agony, they would have married. Only—and this, too, Ronald blames on your mother—he didn't get the letters Alma wrote. And in time, not knowing she had ever experienced a moment of regret over Annie, he loathed her with a deeper loathing than he felt for himself."

Mrs. Hayes's mouth moved dryly. "She deserved it. She earned it."

Mayhew ruffled his notebook. "Eight years went by, and then Alma and Ronald met on the street, spoke, walked together, and talked for about ten minutes. Ronald told me this. He says that he began to wonder if Alma could be the coldhearted creature he had imagined her to be. He asked her to meet him in the deserted house where he had lived with Annie. He wanted to see her reaction. He prepared a room for their meeting in such a way that they could keep it a secret from the other people in the neighborhood. Alma came. She was crying, even after eight years, because of the misery she had given an innocent girl. Ronald Byers was convinced that he and she had again been the victims of a trick to separate them, that the letters she told him of had actually been written and had been stolen from him."

Mrs. Hayes shook her head. "Mother didn't have them any more. She had told me weeks ago that someone had taken them from her room."

"Weeks ago? What date?"

"Oh, in the summer sometime. July, the first part of August. I'm not sure."

"Did she know who had taken them?"

"No. She thought at first that Alma had. I noticed her watching the girl, sitting out in the yard when she thought Alma and Ronald might run into each other, trying to figure out if Ronald had finally seen the letters."

"Did she do anything about getting them back?"

"When Ronald and Alma didn't immediately make up she decided that someone else might have them. She accused us, then somehow fixed on old Mr. Byers. She knew he hadn't liked Alma, that he was as interested in keeping control of the Tellingham estate as she was. You see, there's a small yearly salary that will have to be paid the trustees if the property is ever sold. That gave old Mr. Byers a motive for dragging things out."

"Did she accuse him openly of taking the letters?"

"No. She had Claudia go through his things, but the child didn't find anything. Just got a good whipping from that aunt of hers."

"I see." Mayhew studied his notebook. "What's your opinion?"

She moved uneasily. "I don't know. I can't imagine who has them."

"If they come into your possession will you let me have them?"

"I certainly will." She put force into the words.

Mayhew saw her point. If Mrs. Ruddick had stolen the letters from Ronald, kept them all these years, they were a perfect motive for him or for Alma Tellingham to kill her. Mrs. Hayes would not hesitate to turn such evidence over to Mayhew. It was a clear lead to two people she hated.

Mayhew flipped several pages. "There are a few other things I'd like to clear up. One is the disposal of the estate if all trustees should die."

Mrs. Hayes's eyes gleamed. "You'd better ask Mrs. Tellingham about that."

He let it pass without question. "And the money your mother left. It's a rather sizable amount. What happens to it?"

The gleam departed. "Mr. Hayes and I get it jointly."

"Without any restrictions?"

She made an odd, unwilling noise deep in her throat, half cough and half choking. "Half of it is ours to do with as we want. The other is—is to be kept intact till Claudia is grown. We can use the interest, but the—the principal has to be there for her when she's twenty-one."

Mayhew's genius for looking casual never stood him in better stead. "A lot could happen in the time between then and now. Suppose she never lived to inherit?"

He felt her eyes rake him. "It would be—be lumped in with what we had, in that case."

He let the book fall shut. "I think that covers about everything." He got up, took his hat off a chair.

"My mother's body," she stammered, not moving. "I wondered if we couldn't make some arrangements. . . ."

He nodded. "The inquest is set for tomorrow morning. You may come if you want. Otherwise, since it might be painful, Mr. Hayes can testify as to what you both knew of her movements. After the inquest the body will be released for burial."

She clenched her hands tighter. "Thanks." She sat and watched him as he walked toward the door.

Mrs. Tellingham tried to keep fright out of her eyes when she saw who it was. "Lieutenant Mayhew; that's the name, isn't it? Will you come in?" She was wrapped in a yellow chenille house coat; the color made her skin seem pale, sallow. Her graying hair was pushed high at the temples, giving her features a pulled look. But when she turned to lead Mayhew into the living room she walked evenly, almost precisely.

Alma turned in a chair as they came in. She was seated before a small desk, making out what looked to Mayhew like a shopping list. "How do you do?" she said formally. Her neat brows made a brief frown.

"I'm sorry to disturb you again," Mayhew apologized. "First, I wanted to leave a message for your maid. We'll want her to testify at the inquest tomorrow morning at ten."

"About the shape she says she saw at the cellar window?" Alma made it sound somehow as though it weren't true. "I'll tell her."

"And another question I'd like you to answer." Mayhew looked at a chair, but no invitation was forthcoming; Alma and

Mrs. Tellingham watched him in an odd, stiff silence. "It's about the estate your mother left." He had turned to Mrs. Tellingham. "I'd like to know, please, what would happen to it if all the trustees should die without Miss Tellingham being married."

Mrs. Tellingham grew white; the yellow house coat made a ghastly reflection on chin and cheekbones. "That's rather a far-fetched possibility, isn't it?"

"It's purely hypothetical, of course."

Alma dropped her pencil; it made a sharp click as it hit the hardwood floor.

She bent to retrieve it. "Answer him, Mother. It doesn't amount to anything."

She looked at her daughter, then back to Mayhew. "In the case you—you mention, Alma would inherit the estate. There were no alternate trustees appointed in case these should—should pass away."

"Your daughter would inherit without any restrictions?"

"Ah—not quite. A portion of the property, or the amount realized from its sale, was to be put into a trust fund for their—for their children."

"*Their* children?" Mayhew repeated, not understanding.

"The wording, I believe, was *for the children of said Alma Tellingham and/or Ronald Byers.*" Mrs. Tellingham put her hands behind her, backed toward a window, and leaned on the sill. "You see, even Mother realized that Alma might just possibly marry somebody else."

"Who drew up this will?"

"Mother. She knew just what she wanted."

Mayhew frowned, asked her to repeat the wording. She did so rather reluctantly, and Mayhew could see Alma's intense concentration upon what her mother was saying. "Will you check that for me sometime today?" Mayhew asked when she finished. "I'd like it copied verbatim, if you could manage it."

"The will is on file," Mrs. Tellingham said. "I'll check it if you like." She waited, staring. "Is there something the matter with that part of it?"

"If it reads as you say it does it isn't quite what your mother meant it to be. It doesn't cut out the people she meant it to."

The two women watched him without so much as seeming to breathe. "The word *or* will permit Claudia Byers to inherit that trust fund."

Mrs. Tellingham said something unintelligible and looked at Alma. Alma got up from the little desk.

"I've known it for a long while, Mother. The lawyers told me."

"But Claudia isn't *yours!*" cried Mrs. Tellingham.

"The will says *or Ronald Byers*. She doesn't have to be mine." She stood by the desk; the fine black eyebrows met again. "I was sure that you knew this, Mother. Surely the lawyers told you, too, that day when they came out to arrange about the trusteeships."

Mrs. Tellingham shook her head fiercely, but Mayhew was remembering her reluctance to repeat the wording of the clause.

"I didn't know! How could I? It's fantastic that a child not related to Mother in any way should inherit part of her property. I never dreamed, never imagined . . ." She let her arms drop in a gesture of bewilderment.

"Let's not say any more about it," Alma put in quietly. She glanced at Mayhew. "We'll check this for you and let you know."

Mayhew shook his head. "I'll save you the trouble. Since it's on file I'll have no difficulty looking it up myself."

When he left them he drove downtown to the Hall of Records, left his car in a jammed lot, counted the marble steps in his abstraction. At the Probate Department he was given a copy of the original will, sat down at a table, and made notes at his leisure.

The thing was the result of an ingenious old woman's attempt to keep her precious property out of the hands of her daughter-in-law. That intention shone from every phrase. Each section, from the clause which outlined the cumbersome trusteeship machinery to the final error about the children of Alma and Ronald Byers, was planned for the purpose of outvoting and outmaneuvering Alma's mother. Mayhew got an impression of Barbara Tellingham from reading her will: a shrewd old woman with a one-track mind who had had to live too many years under her daughter-in-law's roof.

Reduced to their minimum, the provisions of the will were fairly simple. Until Alma married the property was to be managed by a board of three trustees: the elder Mr. Byers, Mrs. Ruddick, and Mrs. Tellingham, each to have one vote. When Alma married the property was hers without restrictions. If the members of the board should die before Alma married (what earthly reasoning put this in? Mayhew wondered) she should inherit with restrictions. And here came in the error about the children. In black and white it said *and/or Ronald Byers*. And the child of Ronald Byers was Claudia.

Claudia Byers was, potentially, an heiress.

CHAPTER ELEVEN

MISS RACHEL stood in the soft gloom of the cellar and listened. There was someone in the kitchen above, moving about almost without sound. Occasionally a board creaked; once it seemed she heard the latch of the door that led into the pantry. Miss Rachel expected it to be as all the other intrusions had been: vague, menacing, but inconclusive. Instead, the door at the top of the cellar steps suddenly opened. Mrs. Karov put her head in.

When she saw Miss Rachel a trace of disappointment came into her eyes. For a moment it seemed as though she might withdraw. Then, with a glance behind her, she came through and walked slowly downstairs. She stopped on the bottom step.

"It smells of death here." She drew a long, noisy breath, expelled it lingeringly. "Bad. Very bad. I remember in Russia . . ." She took in the details of the cellar from rafter to floor. "I was Russian when I was a child, and in a cellar near my father's house many people were killed one night. It was over a year before I was in that place, but it still smelled of death."

She came off the steps and looked about curiously. Miss Rachel backed toward the windows over the workbench. Mrs.

Karov's intimacy with the odor and permanence of death was at once fascinating and repulsive.

"Though not the sort of smell you imagine, I think, for the bodies were not there, not even buried under the floor. They had been removed to a mass grave outside the city."

She looked at once gaunt and solid standing there with her thick body wrapped in white, topped by the dark skin and black hair, the eyes oddly alive behind the masklike face. "Were any of your people killed?" Miss Rachel asked, meaning to be sympathetic.

"But no." She seemed surprised. "They were of the secret police. It was good to be of the secret police in those days."

Her gaze swept from left to right, and suddenly she took in the meaning of the space under the stairs.

Miss Rachel didn't wait for Mrs. Karov's further opinions. She went up while the Slavic woman was engaged in getting the closet door open. Until Mrs. Karov was satisfied concerning the odor—and other properties—of the cellar, Miss Rachel wanted to be elsewhere. She went out into the garden.

The fuchsia which she and Claudia had transplanted looked unwell. Its leaves had begun to curl. Miss Rachel brought a pitcher from the kitchen, filled it at an outside faucet, and watered the plant. The dust allowed the water to flow away. Miss Rachel saw that a trench had better be made to hold moisture near the roots.

She dug and patted the ground with her finger tips. She had formed half the circle when something bit through the covering of soil into her flesh. She jerked her fingers up. At the tips of two hung drops of blood, heavy, slow-forming.

She picked up a scrap of twig and probed the earth, and a chunk of glass heaved into sight, razor-edged on all sides, broken roughly into the shape of a star. She poked further; more glass shone out of the dust, all of it sharp and jagged.

Miss Rachel went inside and put peroxide on her cut fingers and bandaged them loosely with cotton. The blood did not sicken her, but the utter meanness of the trick with the fuchsia did. She went and sat in the living room. There had been no glass in the soil when she and Claudia had planted the fuchsia, none in the earth that had clung to the roots when Mr. Hayes handed it across the hedge. Someone had put glass there for the express purpose of cutting the first person who tried to cultivate the soil about the plant. Had it been meant for Claudia?

The thought sent her running to the back door, but there was no sign of the child out of doors.

She had almost forgotten Mrs. Karov, but the slow plod of the woman's big feet sounded on the cellar steps. A moment later Mrs. Karov came into the kitchen. Her face shone and her breath was labored. It was not until later that Miss Rachel was to wonder if the climb from the cellar could account for so much perspiration and disquietude. Mrs. Karov first put her hands behind her and then brought them forth as if to display them. Miss Rachel sought mentally for a way to describe the act. It was as though Mrs. Karov were bothered by the memory of something she had recently held, about which she wanted Miss Rachel to know nothing.

"It is bad down there," Mrs. Karov said, advancing. "You do not go down much, yes? I think it is better you do not."

Miss Rachel, still stung by the pain in her fingers, her mind set on the puzzle of the glass in the soil about the fuchsia, paid little conscious heed to the meaning behind the singsong words. She was anxious for Mrs. Karov to leave. She felt ill, in need of lying down.

"There is still a bad feeling down there," Mrs. Karov continued. "It is not so much a smell of death which has been as that which is to be." The black eyes shone; a little mustache of perspiration frosted Mrs. Karov's upper lip. She put a hand on Miss Rachel's frail one. "I would not go into the cellar if I were you."

The grammatically correct words spoken in the outlandish voice penetrated Miss Rachel's abstraction. She jerked her hand away. Mrs. Karov's gaze dropped to the bandages.

"You have hurt yourself?"

Miss Rachel took up a stand by the door leading into the passageway. "A little. It doesn't amount to anything."

"Very bad." Mrs. Karov went slowly to the other door and opened it. She waited, as if wanting some invitation to stay, but Miss Rachel gave her none.

Miss Rachel watched the stocky figure pick its way through the neglected rose garden and the overgrown alley to emerge on the smooth back lawn of the Tellingham house. As soon as Mrs. Karov reached the borders of the lawn a waiting figure appeared at the rear door. It looked to Miss Rachel like Mrs. Tellingham. She was in a yellow robe; the face behind the pane was dead white, sick. Miss Rachel wondered what sort of shock she could have had to make her look so. A car started with a sudden roar on the other street; Miss Rachel recognized Mayhew's car as it sped away.

She wondered what his business with the Tellinghams had been, whether it accounted for the distress of Mrs. Tellingham.

The Slavic maid stopped on the grass and looked at Mrs. Tellingham, and Mrs. Tellingham looked back. The two women seemed to measure each other. There was a touch of defiance in the way Mrs. Tellingham opened the door and stepped out upon the porch. And still Mrs. Karov stared; with what expression Miss Rachel could not even guess.

The sunlight shimmered in the space above the roses, reflected in a white glare from the white cement drive at the rear of the Tellingham house. Miss Rachel's eyes stung; her fingers ached. She was possessed with a sudden weariness with all of it.

She went upstairs and lay down, and then for a while she slept.

She was bothered by dreams in which fantastic questions rolled in upon her from the depths of a gray fog. There was almost the effect of a loud-speaker, and the things asked by the unknown voice set her pulses hammering, brought cold perspiration out upon her scalp.

What, asked the voice, *did Mrs. Karov find in the cellar and then decide not to bring up with her?*

Heavens, answered Miss Rachel, *did she?*

The voice accused her of having already known it, and Miss Rachel examined a dreamy conscience for something she hadn't known she had known.

Who's trying to hurt Claudia?

I don't know, Miss Rachel replied. *How could I?*

Of course you know, the voice said. *Your intuition has told you.*

Through the enveloping gray fog Miss Rachel went hunting for her intuition, and when she found it, it turned out to be a blue stone with an eyelike stare set in a fringe of pearls. Miss Rachel clutched it, found it cold. If this was intuition it was remarkably little help.

In her dream she walked on and on through the fog while the loud-speaker boomed out at her.

Why was the weapon used to kill Mrs. Ruddick left in your room? Can't you see what's going to happen?

What about your intuition?

Miss Rachel had no answers for these. The roar of the voice was deafening.

It might help, she thought, to stuff some of the fog into her ear. She woke with a handful of pillow, pressing it against her head. And in the first moment of waking she knew that the loud-speaker voice hadn't been all a dream. A blare of sound drifted from the lower part of the house in through the open door of her bedroom.

She pulled on her shoes quickly, staring with sleepy eyes at the room. The sunlight had a mellow afternoon tint to it. In the uneven distances of the mirror she found herself reflected, eyes dull and wide and with a patch of red in each cheek.

She ran downstairs and into the living room, where the radio, turned screamingly high, boomed forth an interminable commercial. Her ears ached, held the sound even after she had cut it off abruptly by turning the knob. She rubbed her head, tried to remember the long dream she had had, the dream about the fog and the loud, demanding voice that flung questions at her. The radio had supplied the background, of course; her mind had used the exterior voice to frame questions of its own making.

Someone was pounding at the front door.

She felt her mind shake with the impact of the thudding. She wished she could awake, really come alive, instead of living in this queer continuation of a dream. When she went into the hall the sunlight struck through the dust motes with a queer effect of fog, and the pounding on the door seemed but another act of the mysterious being who had shouted so loudly before.

The thick hinges creaked, and Miss Rachel found herself

looking out at Mayhew, a Mayhew who barked without any preliminary: "What's going on in here?"

Miss Rachel stepped back, and he came forward out of the sun. "What was that infernal racket that stopped a minute ago?"

"The radio?" she offered.

He looked at her curiously. "It could have been."

She led the way into the living room, still with a core of drowsiness in her thoughts. "I was having a nap upstairs, and somehow the volume was increased. . . . You know how these old sets are."

"You had turned the radio on before you went up to sleep?"

"I suppose that I did."

He walked to the radio and twisted the dials thoughtfully. A slow hum announced the set's warming up; then a voice began to babble. Mayhew turned the volume control, experimenting with it. The knob controlling the volume moved scratchily, with difficulty. In no way did the set fail to respond to the movements of the knob.

"This didn't turn itself up accidentally." He watched Miss Rachel's puzzlement. "Are you sure you didn't turn it up yourself?"

"I don't believe that I even had it on," she decided.

Miss Rachel could see that his thoughts went abruptly elsewhere. He was no longer interested in the radio; he was interested in the use to which it had been put. She cast about, drove the last vestiges of sleep out of her mind, trying to keep ahead of him.

Miss Rachel was scarcely more than a step behind when he started for the cellar.

He stopped in the pantry (she had known that he would) and looked back at her with what she knew he thought was diplomacy.

"Hadn't you better wait here for a minute?"

She saw that he was going to be stubborn if she persisted in following, so she folded her hands and looked innocent. "Should I?"

"Please. I'll call you if it's all right."

His large back vanished through the cellar door, and Miss Rachel came to life and went after it. She put an eye to the crack. Mayhew was halfway down the stairs, stock-still, looking at the floor. Miss Rachel couldn't make out what he was watching. He must have stood that way, quiet, immobile, for half a minute. Then he ran down and out of her range of vision.

Miss Rachel hooked one of her bandaged finger tips into the door and pulled it slightly. She caught sight of Mayhew's foot, his bent back. He was kneeling down over in the direction of the furnace.

"Miss Murdock!" Mayhew boomed. "Come here!"

She almost fell over herself getting in upon the stairs, and then Mayhew said: "Stop! Don't come down. I want you to go next door and use their telephone to call the doctor. Get an ambulance too. Tell them to bring a blood-transfusion apparatus and supply of plasma. And tell them, for the love of God, to hurry!"

Miss Rachel began automatically to run because she is fundamentally trustful of Lieutenant Mayhew's decisions, but her mind bubbled with confusion. There had been something on the floor behind Mayhew's figure, something big and sprawled and formless.

Outside the front door she turned toward the Byers house and then brought up short. She remembered Bernice Byers' caustic criticism on the occasion of her previous use of their phone. For an instant that might have been a year Miss Rachel stood and debated with herself. It was Mrs. Hayes who solved her problem, coming out on the front porch of the other house to shake a small rug over the banister.

Miss Rachel ran toward her. "Could I use your telephone? It's an emergency; Lieutenant Mayhew sent me."

Mrs. Hayes let the rug slide out of her large capable-looking hands and fixed on Miss Rachel a look of active dislike. "If you must," she said grudgingly. She marked with a military stride, ushering Miss Rachel into the hall.

She stood over Miss Rachel when the little old lady tried to dial the police, and in the gloom of the hall Miss Rachel saw her hands move oddly, either in anger or from a desire to take the telephone out of Miss Rachel's fumbling fingers and do the job herself.

The voice of the law had just crackled in her ear when Mayhew strode in at the door, "Excuse me. I'll take it." He reached past Miss Rachel, lifted the French-style receiver toward his ear. "Mayhew speaking. Cancel the order for the blood-transfusion preparations, if you had one. Send the homicide men." He gave the address and further directions briefly.

Then he put down the receiver and looked at Mrs. Hayes. "Is your husband here now?"

"I think so." She walked to the stairs that led up from the entryway and bellowed: "Bill! Oh, Bill!"

Mr. Hayes could be heard running; then he thrust his face over the rail of the upper floor and said, "Yes, dear?"

"Have you both been here during the last fifteen minutes?" Mayhew asked.

"Certainly," said Mrs. Hayes.

"Within sight of each other?"

Her eye wavered. "Well, we were more or less around. I

think Bill's been upstairs, except when he went out to—to—"
She paused, glanced up at the round face at the top of the banister. "Just what did you do when you went out about twenty minutes ago, Bill? You were awfully quiet out there in the back yard."

Bill's mouth made sputtering sounds. "But I *didn't* go out! *I didn't!*" He swallowed, choked, got his voice back. "You're making it up! It isn't true!"

A cloud crossed her military calm. "Very well," she muttered. "Perhaps you didn't."

Mayhew could scarcely endure to wait; he said, "See that both of you stay here for the present," and ran out. Miss Rachel hurried after, not without the sense of a storm brewing in the Hayes household.

The lieutenant went back into Miss Rachel's house, plunged through directly to the cellar, and went down. He forgot to warn her, and Miss Rachel made bold to follow.

She, too, stopped on the stairs at first sight of the thing on the floor.

Spread out oddly like a big broken animal, her torso covered by a dark blue coat, her face and hands smeared with blood, and her glassy eyes looking straight up into Miss Rachel's, lay the Slavic maid, Mrs. Karov.

CHAPTER TWELVE

MAYHEW PULLED the collar of the dark coat up to shut out the sight of Mrs. Karov's face and then ran back upstairs toward Miss Rachel.

"This thing is a matter of minutes," he jerked out. "Will you stay here while I check on the people in the other houses?"

She nodded; he didn't wait to see but went past with a bound. Miss Rachel started upstairs, and at the same moment that Mayhew flung the back door shut behind him her eye lit again on the coat that covered Mrs. Karov.

She went down slowly to the cellar floor and approached Mrs. Karov's body. The coat was of medium length, dark, inconspicuous. Miss Rachel could not decide whether it was a man's coat or a woman's. But the buttons were unmistakable. She bent down, suddenly and dreadfully aware of what Mrs. Karov must have meant by the smell of death, and turned the hem of her petticoat so that the button she had found wedged in the trellis showed as a dark spot on the snowy cotton. She held it toward the buttons on the coat.

They were of the same mold, the same material—identical.

With a growing sense of excitement she counted the buttons of the coat, counted the buttonholes. For a moment, so sure had she been of her clue, she failed to realize what she had found. Then the bottom dropped out of her excitement. For every buttonhole had its corresponding button, from top to hem, collar, pocket, and belt. There were eight buttonholes. There were eight buttons. Miss Rachel let her petticoat drop.

So the button she had found in the trellis didn't really mean anything, after all. Here was the coat it logically belonged upon—and there weren't any buttons missing off it.

She straightened, looking about at the cellar, wondering now what could have brought the Tellingham maid back here. The door to the cubicle where Mrs. Ruddick had died was open; Miss Rachel peeped in, but the closet's walls and floor were bare. Even the little pile of rusty tools at the door had been removed—doubtless in hopes that some shred of the murderer's clothing might have caught in them.

The corner behind the furnace was a shadowy hole into which she ventured with some reluctance. The rat's nest was gone, the space swept clean by Mayhew's men. The brick walls and the dark hulk of the furnace gave off a feeling of coolness. But there seemed to be nothing in which Mrs. Karov would have found interest.

She left the cellar and went up to the kitchen and waited. Presently a squad car arrived; men trooped through into the pantry, carrying the paraphernalia of the homicide department, and Miss Rachel went to the living room to be out of the way.

She had not expected to find anyone here, and when she first caught sight of Mrs. Tellingham bent over on the davenport, sobbing into Alma's lap, she had a sense of incongruity and shock. Alma was white, her dark eyes dull, as though an artist had thumbed them in with charcoal, and one hand stroked her mother's hair mechanically, over and over. She was staring at something on the opposite wall. Rounding the doorframe, Miss Rachel saw that the something was Ronald Byers. He was looking back at Alma, and something in his eyes defied and resented the accusation in hers.

"That's it," Miss Rachel said to herself, "Alma's telling him he did it, and he's trying to say that he didn't."

Claudia sat in a corner, watchful, not quite understanding Mrs. Tellingham's grief or her father's preoccupation with Alma. Beside Claudia was Bernice Byers, her spinster's mouth quite thin, her back stiff as a poker. Claudia's grandfather completed the group. He looked ill at ease and kept running a wiry hand through his white hair, rubbing his palm against his chin, making all sorts of nervous gestures to distract himself from his worry.

The Hayeses were ushered through the doorway, Mayhew following. Mr. Hayes's round face was red, his eyes ready to pop.

"I *didn't* go outside!" he was saying loudly. "She's made that up. I've been upstairs practically all day, especially during the last couple of hours."

Mrs. Hayes looked straight ahead, took a chair without saying anything. Her expression gave nothing away; it was as impenetrable as that of a general on a parade ground.

When the group was seated, mutual glances of recrimination exchanged, and the attention finally directed toward Mayhew he moved forward a step or so from the doorway and spoke.

"When I first discovered Mrs. Karov some twenty-five minutes ago"—he glanced at his watch—"she was still alive. She had been stabbed only a few minutes before. I think you can therefore see how important it is for me to have an exact account of the movements of each one of you—especially during the past hour." He glanced toward Mr. Hayes, who was literally jumping up and down in his chair. "Yours, please."

"I was in the house, upstairs, puttering in my room. I don't care what *she* says." He all but bared his teeth in the direction of his wife. "That's where I was, and I'll stick to it!"

Mayhew glanced at Mrs. Hayes. "And you?"

"I was indoors." She said it calmly, placidly. "I was dusting the front hallway."

"Could Mr. Hayes have gone outdoors without your seeing him?"

"He could have used the kitchen stairs." She ignored his glaring anger. "As a matter of fact, I did hear the kitchen door close just about five minutes or so before I went out on the porch and saw Miss Murdock on the sidewalk."

"You were within sight of a clock?"

"No. I just judged the time."

"Could you hear the noise of Miss Murdock's radio?"

"Very plainly. I wonder anyone would want such a racket in the house."

"Did the sound of your back door closing come before or after you first heard the radio?"

She paused and let Mayhew's question sink in. "Before, as nearly as I remember."

Mayhew glanced at his watch. "Will you let me know when you think five minutes have passed?"

She flushed a little, as though he had implied an untruth in her statement about the time, but Mayhew didn't wait for her reaction. He turned to Mrs. Tellingham. At his question she

raised herself and dried her eyes. "I've been in the house all afternoon. I was taking a nap, but I woke about a half-hour ago,
and since then I've read a story or so in a magazine."

"Can you tell me anything about Mrs. Karov's movements
during the afternoon?"

"I'm afraid not. She has—*had*—two hours free every day,
and she usually rested or did that odd European needlework she
was so fond of. I—I don't know what she did today, except that
of course she must have come here."

Mayhew looked at Alma. "I was in my room," she said
simply.

"Does your room overlook the rear of this house?" From her
story about the window Miss Rachel knew that Mayhew already had the answer to this question.

"I was sitting with my back to the window. I was reading
recipes, trying to find something that would appeal to Mother
for dinner. I haven't any idea of how long I sat there or of anything which went on over here."

Mayhew tried to hide his impatience, but Miss Rachel saw
it gain on him, saw his dislike for this situation where everyone
claimed to be at home, where no one could vouch for the other,
where one was lying—because *someone*, one of them, had come
here and murdered Mrs. Karov.

He turned toward the group against the other wall, and
Ronald Byers put himself forth as spokesman. "I'm sure you
needn't suspect any of us, Lieutenant. What earthly motive
could my sister or I or my father have in murdering this woman?
In spite of the fact that she had lived in a nearby house for years,
we scarcely knew her. Her interests, her movements, in no way
met ours."

"The motive for the murder of Mrs. Karov is a rather obvious one," Mayhew answered. "She was, if you remember her statement, the only person who had seen the murderer of Mrs. Ruddick."

"But the way she described the figure," Bernice put in, "was so vague that I—"

Mayhew cut in: "Detailed description is hard for a woman of Mrs. Karov's type, but there was nothing wrong with her eyes. She was a constant menace to the murderer because she might at any time recall or recognize something familiar, some characteristic she hadn't been able to describe in words."

The group let the words sink in, and the shock and fear that were so near the surface in all of them showed a little more plainly. Alma quit stroking her mother's hand which she had taken between her own, and Mrs. Tellingham drew away and shivered. Ronald Byers stared at his sister with a troubled look. Grandpa put his fingers together and blew across their tips as though he were sounding some invisible bugle. Mr. Hayes gulped, swallowed. Only Mrs. Hayes retained her majestic calm.

She said: "The Russian woman was a queer one. If she had seen the murderer again and recognized him there's no telling what she might have done. She might have called the police and she might not. She'd be just as apt to go up to his face and accuse him."

"She had been very secretive of late," Mrs. Tellingham offered with an air of having to say something.

"I had the impression," Alma said slowly, "that she had been looking for something. She lost a ring about two years ago. I think she suspected someone of taking it. At any rate, she went around in a peculiar, watchful way. And that's how she's been recently since Mrs. Ruddick died."

"Do you remember any specific remarks she made?" Mayhew asked.

Alma shook her head. "It was a general impression I got from her actions, not any one specific thing."

Grandpa gripped the arms of his chair and leaned forward. "Aren't you jumping to conclusions a little, Lieutenant? Not meaning any criticism, of course, you being the police and all, but couldn't Mrs. Ruddick and Mrs. Karov have been killed by somebody who isn't here, some prowler, maybe?"

The room was dead quiet. Some of the people looked at Grandpa with a trace of hope. Others—Mrs. Hayes, Bernice Byers, Mrs. Tellingham—were hard put to hide their impatience at the silly statement.

Mayhew said calmly: "Until we find some trace of a stranger's having been in this neighborhood, and until we can disprove what seems to have been strong motive in the case of Mrs. Ruddick's murder, we will have to proceed as we are, questioning you people who knew or were in contact with the dead women."

"I still don't see . . ." Grandpa's voice dropped; he lifted his hands aimlessly. "Oh, all right. I guess you know what you're doing."

Mayhew took advantage of the moment to step out into the hall and to receive from a passing officer a paper-wrapped slender object, which he brought in and displayed. He held it, still in its paper, by the tip of the blade. "Anyone recognize this?"

There was a slow hiss from Mr. Hayes, dead silence from Mrs. Hayes. The long knife glittered in the late sunlight; a reflected beam passed over Ronald Byers' face, and he shut his eyes against it.

Mrs. Hayes said at last: "It's my butcher knife."

"How long since you've missed it?" Mayhew asked practically.

"I haven't." She wet her lips slowly. "I mean, I thought it was still in the kitchen at home."

"You used it today?"

"At lunch." She quit looking at Mayhew, and her eyes crept around until they rested on her husband, who promptly shuddered. "I remember using it to cut some ham. Bill sharpened it for me. As far as I know, it was left lying on the sink."

"And you, Mr. Hayes?"

Words literally burst from him. "I sharpened it, like she says, brought it in to her, and put it down. That's all I know. I didn't see it after lunch."

"Did you," Mayhew asked carefully, "while you were upstairs, hear a sound as though someone had left your house by the kitchen door?"

A look of obvious cunning came into Mr. Hayes's face. "I think I did." Miss Rachel could see his point. If the knife had somehow traveled from the Hayes kitchen to her cellar, there to kill Mrs. Karov, it was much better for Mr. Hayes to admit the presence of a prowler than to deny he had heard anything.

Mrs. Hayes broke in with, "I think it's been about five minutes since you asked me to judge the time."

Mayhew glanced at his watch but said nothing, to Mrs. Hayes's open disappointment.

There was, after that, a session of questions about the knife which produced nothing for Mayhew. No one had seen anyone leave the Hayes rear door carrying the butcher knife. No one had seen anyone leave Miss Rachel's house after the radio had been turned high, though several noticed the increased sound.

It was nearly sunset when Mayhew dismissed them and went

to see what was being done in the cellar. Miss Rachel remained alone in the living room. She was excessively tired, and she was beginning to be genuinely afraid, not an easily recognizable surface emotion, but a deep cold uneasiness like the starting up of an interior freezing machine. While she sat and listened to the faraway thumps from the cellar, she summarized a few ideas about the murder of Mrs. Karov, both from Mayhew's point of view and from her own.

She thought that Mayhew had tentatively accepted Mrs. Hayes's statement of having heard someone go out of the kitchen shortly before Mrs. Karov had been murdered. Doubtless he figured that the murderer had been in the Hayes house on some mission of spying or prowling, had seen Mrs. Karov sneak in at the rear next door, had snatched up the butcher knife, and in his hurry at leaving had made the sound Mrs. Hayes claimed to have heard. Proceeding next door, the murderer had followed Mrs. Karov into the cellar (what would she be doing there, incidentally, to be so engrossed as to allow someone to creep up on her with a butcher knife?) and had there slaughtered her. Leaving, he had turned the radio up into an unnaturally loud screech to cover the death cries of Mrs. Karov.

That was how Mayhew would figure it.

As for herself, she would have liked to have pricked the unnatural calm with which Mrs. Hayes had withstood the afternoon's events.

Suppose Mrs. Hayes, instead of dusting the front hall, had herself been in the kitchen, had seen Mrs. Karov go into Miss Rachel's house, and had followed and done the murder? It was bad from the point of motive. Why should Mrs. Hayes have killed Mrs. Karov, unless Mrs. Karov had first accused the other woman as the murderer of her mother? And there was no proof that Mrs. Karov had gone anywhere but into Miss Rachel's cellar.

Mayhew came back in the middle of her meditations and sat down. "Look," he began abruptly. "If you won't go back home to your sister, for the love of Pete, at least get out of this house. Rent a room in the neighborhood somewhere. I'm not suggesting any of the other three houses in this block, because I'm pretty sure that in one of them is the murderer, and I don't want you exposed to him. But go somewhere else at night. I get the creeps thinking of you alone here."

Miss Rachel let a moment pass discreetly. "Were there any fingerprints on the radio or the knife handle?"

He looked disgusted, but he did answer. "Nothing. Must have worn gloves."

"What about that dark coat on Mrs. Karov?"

He nodded toward the hall. "I'm going now to check with the Tellinghams on that point. It isn't the kind of coat I'd expect the woman to wear. It's old but it's expensive, and, to start with, it's a man's coat, though a woman like her mightn't have cared about that." He got up. "You will get another place for tonight, won't you?"

"I think I'd better," she agreed.

"A little distance away."

"A little." She didn't go on to say how little.

"I'll see you in an hour or so and give you a lift." He walked out through the front door into a red sunset. Miss Rachel kept still until his footsteps had died away. Then she made haste into the cellar.

The detectives had tidied the place in their thorough stripping. There were now no rat's nest, no cobwebs, no odds and ends of trash. The only spot with any mystery left in it was the dark corner behind the furnace. Miss Rachel tripped in, came out at the other side, went back, and for lack of anything more exciting to do began feeling the brick wall.

There wouldn't be apt to be anything at eye level; that would be obvious and easy to spot. She let her fingers stray low and then high, then stood on tiptoe as she felt a jutting edge. She pulled; two bricks fastened with cement came out together with a scraping noise.

Chills ran over her. She paused with the bricks half removed, and for a horrid moment she thought that she had heard someone in the kitchen. Complete silence reassured her. She put a hand into the hole where the bricks had been. A crackle of paper answered the touch of a nail. She drew forth a letter—then another.

She could have hugged herself, in spite of the terror which the gloomy cellar was beginning to raise in her. She had found them—the letters that Mayhew and his men had missed, the letters that Mrs. Ruddick and Mrs. Karov must have searched for just before . . .

Her heart lurched and seemed to stop.

There was blood, a fresh bright smear of it, right across the face of the topmost letter, and there was also—and definitely—somebody on the stairs.

CHAPTER THIRTEEN

MISS RACHEL's first impulses were to run, to scream, to make such an unearthly racket that the thing on the stairs would go away without any trouble. She opened her mouth to discover that her throat was paralyzed. The letters dropped from her fingers. She knew with a dreadful certainty that this was what must have happened to Mrs. Ruddick and Mrs. Karov, a last-minute paralysis that made them helpless.

She did manage to totter out from behind the furnace with an idea of meeting death in the open, with at least the last flickerings of daylight in which to see the world she was about to leave. Round-eyed, she stared at the figure on the stairs.

Mrs. Hayes came down another step, forced her mouth into a smile that all but cracked it. "We—ah—my husband and I were worried about you. Bill suggested that we ask you if you'd like to stay the night with us. You'll—you'll be frightened here all by yourself."

She was ignoring the fact that she had located Miss Rachel in the cellar where the crimes had been committed, not a place to find a timid woman. Miss Rachel stifled a retort about people who creep up on one without warning; it was, after all, just the opportunity she wanted.

"It's very thoughtful of you," she said; mentally she added, *If you take another step I'll start screaming.*

Mrs. Hayes, though, actually ascended a step or so, as though she might be afraid of the cellar.

"Then we can expect you?" she asked. The smile was wearing thin, and something new was peering from under it; what the new expression was, Miss Rachel could not quite decide. Could it be anticipation?

"I'll be over in about an hour," Miss Rachel promised.

Mrs. Hayes went up to the top of the stairs. "Plan to have dinner with us," she said and disappeared.

Miss Rachel wanted to stand still and think about the odd behavior of Mrs. Hayes, the strange burst of friendship where before had been military stiffness; but, more than that, she wanted those letters. She scurried back behind the furnace and picked them off the floor. The smear of blood had picked up some particles of dust, obscuring the written address, but they were the same letters, nevertheless, which she had first seen in the metal box in the hole above the stairs.

She quite shamelessly read both of them.

RONNIE, MY DEAR: (She'd read part of this before.)

It is much too late to try to explain; too late, too, for you to understand how I feel—my abasement and agony. Death is so final, so complete, such an utter end of everything. There is now no way that I can talk to Annie and try, even a little, to win her forgiveness for what I have done to her. My very soul cries, "Annie, I was cruel, but it was a thoughtless cruelty. I took out on you the revenge I felt for another. Forgive, Annie, because I didn't know until it was too late just what I was doing."

And then, of course, I come again to the realization that An-

nie doesn't answer because she is dead and that all my grief won't bring her back again. If she could come back, Ronnie, I would never see you again. Giving up our love would be small price for the happiness of a child who never did us any harm, who was just the tool of a conniving old woman wrapped up in her own selfish schemes—a child that you and I, Ronnie, made miserable during the last year she lived.

Good-by, my dear. I wanted you to know how I felt because, wherever Annie is, you are my only link to her.

ALMA

Miss Rachel put the letter back into its blood-smeared envelope and took time, before opening the other, to dab at her eyes with her finger tips.

RONALD: (So much more formal—Miss Rachel glanced at the date. It was later than the first by eleven days.)

Yesterday when we met and I spoke to you, you didn't answer. Did you really not see me?

I thought that there was a look of loathing in your eyes. Surely, Ronald, you won't add your hatred to what I have already gone through since Annie died. I admit, as I did in the other letter I wrote you, that I was inhumanly thoughtless and cruel; but you should know, more than anyone, what motives led me into such behavior.

Won't you write me, even a line, to let me know that you received my letter? I would then at least feel that someone knew and understood my grief. Don't be afraid that I will intrude on you or try to force myself into a situation which must be painful in the extreme. I will never speak to you again, unless you speak first to me.

ALMA

The eight-year-old sheets were dry and crisp. Miss Rachel folded them together, and they made a soft crackle as she slipped them into the envelope. She made a final exploration of the cubbyhole behind the bricks, and when it proved empty she put the bricks into place and went upstairs.

She waited a long while before Mayhew came, still lugging the dark coat that had covered Mrs. Karov. He sat in one of her rickety chairs and, lights now being necessary because it had grown dark, read the letters under an overhead bulb.

He seemed more interested in the bloodstain than in the contents of the letters. "This smear more or less proves that Mrs. Karov had located the letters and had them with her when she died. The blood is too fresh to have been Mrs. Ruddick's. Tests will type the blood, of course." He put the letters carefully into an inside pocket.

"I suppose it wouldn't be according to police procedure to let Ronald Byers see them first."

"I think he could see them." Mayhew was watchful. "What do you think we'd get out of it?"

"I don't know." She frowned, staring at the square of white that shone out from between Mayhew's big fingers. "The letters have some sort of connection with the murders, else Mrs. Ruddick and Mrs. Karov wouldn't have been killed while they were hunting for them."

"Perhaps," Mayhew suggested heavily, "Ronald Byers doesn't need to be shown these letters."

"You mean that he's already seen them?"

"If they are a part of the crime they connect him with it. The whole point of their being hidden was to keep him from seeing them."

To herself Miss Rachel admitted his logic. One construction of the crime could be that Ronald had come across Mrs. Ruddick just as she retrieved the letters which had been taken from her and hidden in the cellar. Realizing that she had ruined eight years of his life so far as his love for Alma was concerned, he had murdered her in rage and revenge and rehidden the letters to keep his motive out of sight. Then, suspecting that Mrs. Karov might eventually recognize him as the figure in the dark coat she had glimpsed at the cellar window and knowing, also, that she was on the trail of the hidden letters, he had killed her too.

That explained everything—except one point. Who had taken the letters from old Mrs. Ruddick in the first place?

Mayhew was getting ready to leave her. Miss Rachel's eye fell on the coat which he had put across a chair.

"What did the Tellinghams say about *that?*" She pointed daintily.

Mayhew threw it a glance. "It's an old coat Mrs. Karov has had for several years. Mrs. Tellingham doesn't know where she got it, thinks it might have been at a rummage sale. I've an idea she wore it when she wanted to be inconspicuous. It's dark and plain-cut and wouldn't attract much attention."

"There doesn't seem to be much blood on it," Miss Rachel observed.

"No, there isn't. It must have been thrown over her after she was killed."

"Just how was she killed? You said something about stabbing, but you didn't give any details."

"She was stabbed first in the back and then in the throat. According to the doctor, neither wound would prove immediately fatal. The murderer must have left her still alive, though of course rapidly bleeding to death. It accounts for your radio being turned up, a piece of unheard-of brutal audacity if I ever saw one. The radio would cover any sounds Mrs. Karov might make. It would also, of course, awaken you. The murderer made quick work of getting out afterward."

"It almost looks—" Miss Rachel said and stopped. She had been about to say that Mrs. Hayes's having had a hand in the murder was almost inevitable. She had been, by her own admission, in the front hall of her house, a good post from which to watch for an opportunity for entering next door, an excellent place into which to duck quickly after the deed was done.

"Yes?" Mayhew asked.

"I don't know. I wish the Tellinghams had remembered where Mrs. Karov got that coat." Miss Rachel turned her attention on the folded garment.

Mayhew, naturally, didn't know why she was interested in it. "It doesn't seem to have played much of a part in the crime, beyond the fact that Mrs. Karov wore it over here."

Miss Rachel bit her lip. For the second time she wished she could tell Mayhew about the button she had found in the trellis. *It* was the reason she was puzzled over the coat. It was like putting together a jigsaw-puzzle picture of a horse and finding two tails and only one rump to hang them on. The button sewn to her petticoat hem was identical with those on Mrs. Karov's coat. It should rightfully have been *off* that coat, but it wasn't. It had come off the coat of someone Miss Rachel had presumed was the murderer.

A shrewd idea came into Miss Rachel's mind. This coat might not be Mrs. Karov's at all! People paid little attention to the clothes worn by their servants; the Tellinghams could be mistaken, and Mrs. Karov's coat could be hanging at this moment in her closet! *This* might be the murderer's coat, left behind because of bloodstains or something, the button which had been torn off on the trellis replaced by a new one!

She was so anxious to pursue the idea that she all but pushed Mayhew out of the door.

The last thing he said was, "And you're not staying here tonight?"

"Certainly not!"

Rid of him, she ran through the house to the back door and slipped out into the garden. She snagged her hose getting through the rosebushes, almost fell in the ruts of the alley. But once on the smooth lawn of the Tellingham yard, she went swiftly and quietly to the back door.

There was light reflected into the Tellingham kitchen from the front part of the house. Miss Rachel could make out the objects in the large square room—the stove, cupboards, sink, worktable, and breakfast corner. She tried the knob, and the door moved silently inward, and she slid in past it.

This was trespassing, and Miss Rachel felt a sting of guilt as she slipped over to the door that let into the other part of the house.

Here she found a semilighted hallway with stairs going up into darkness at the right and, directly across, another door which showed a dining-and-living room with Alma and Mrs. Tellingham at its far end.

Mrs. Tellingham was saying something in a high-pitched, nervous tone. Miss Rachel caught the words, ". . . I won't stand for it. Mother didn't mean it to be that way. It's got to be *stopped!*"

"Please don't get so excited, Mother." Alma sounded exhausted. "We can't change things now."

"Can't we, though!" Mrs. Tellingham flung about in her chair; the face she turned in Miss Rachel's direction could have belonged to a mad-woman.

Miss Rachel knew that a situation so charged with excitement couldn't last long. One of the women would blow up or collapse and both of them separate, probably to go to their rooms upstairs. She had, perforce, to hurry. Alma's voice followed her as she went up the carpeted stairway.

Alma said, "You don't know what you're saying." And Mrs. Tellingham answered through rising sobs.

The upper hall was dark, but there was a light in one of the rooms. Miss Rachel opened the door and peeped in. A glance showed that it belonged to Mrs. Tellingham. Her yellow house coat was thrown across the bed; there was a picture on the dressing table of a man about fifty who looked vaguely like Alma in a masculine fashion, and a bottle of smelling salts sat on the night stand.

Miss Rachel withdrew, leaving the door open a trifle so that she could see her way about the hall.

The second room, directly across, was that with windows which faced Miss Rachel's back door. Across the alley shone Miss Rachel's kitchen light with the straggling maze of the rose garden below, the branches of the rosebushes like a nest of skinny arms in the half glow from the house. Miss Rachel paused long enough at the window to glance across; then in the dimness her eye fell on a chair with a book thrown down upon its cushion.

She went to the light switch and pushed it, then went back to examine the book. It was a book of recipes, the pages open at a collection of gelatine puddings. She recalled Alma's story to

Mayhew—that at the time Mrs. Karov must have been killed she had been in her room looking for something appetizing to prepare for dinner.

Urged by some odd compulsion, Miss Rachel took up the book and sat down in the chair.

Across the room, facing her, the dressing-table mirror showed the open window, the flapping draperies. Miss Rachel got up, turned off the light, went back to the chair. Now, instead of a square of darkness, the mirror reflected Miss Rachel's back door as she had seen it by looking out a moment or two before, with light shining from the panes over the sink and in the upper half of the door, and even a portion of the rose garden.

If Alma Tellingham had sat here when she said she had, she could scarcely have missed seeing the murderer go into Miss Rachel's house!

Miss Rachel rearranged the book, closed the door when she went out. She felt worse than afraid; she felt shaken, unsure of herself. For until now she had seen Alma as a headstrong but fundamentally honest young woman, and now she knew that Alma was a liar!

The next door that she tried proved to be the bathroom; the last (wouldn't it be? she thought wryly) was the one she had come to see—Mrs. Karov's.

She listened before going in. There was no sign that Alma or her mother meant as yet to come upstairs. Miss Rachel shut the door softly behind her, felt for the light switch along the wall.

The wallpaper had a slick feel to it, as though Mrs. Karov might have come up many a night with her hands greasy with dishwater and slid her big palm back and forth, just as Miss Rachel was doing now. The thought gave Miss Rachel a suddenly clear vision of Mrs. Karov, of her big, placid Slavic face, her inscrutable eyes, her barrel-like body. The way Mrs. Karov had talked, slowly and with a heavy accent, came back to her, and the memory of Mrs. Karov's breath stirred in her face.

Miss Rachel's fingers found the light switch and then lost it, and when she found it again there was something wrong about it. Something terribly wrong. There was a leathery, rounding thing covering the middle of it. And at the same instant she knew that the breath that stirred toward her out of the dark belonged not to the memory of Mrs. Karov but to somebody very much alive.

Miss Rachel swallowed her heart.

There was a hand covering the light switch, a hand in a suède glove!

CHAPTER FOURTEEN

It is said that a drowning person remembers as in a flash the details of his whole life, and Miss Rachel believes this, because as she stood there with her fingers touching that other hand in the dark, a review of the last three days went through her mind with the speed of a nightmare.

She recalled the ghastliness of the dead toad, Claudia's hidden tears, Ronald Byers on the stairs of her house with a gun in his hand, Mrs. Ruddick's dead face staring up out of gloom, the button hanging by a tag of thread in the vine, Mrs. Karov's secretive blank eyes—and much more. The whole dreadful panorama of a crime, in fact. And she opened her mouth to cry out.

What happened next didn't come connectedly into her memory. There was a murmur of speech from the hall. That would be Alma and her mother coming upstairs. Miss Rachel, in that split second of listening, caught a sob, a fragment of angry talk. Whether this came before or after the blow that whistled at her from out of the dark, she could never remember. She may have heard the voices while she was falling, even in a moment of consciousness after she had hit the floor. At any rate, the cry never got out of her. It was cut off by a blow from that other hand, the one not under hers on the light switch. The murderer, if murderer it was, had been ready. The hand contained a heavy old-fashioned glass inkwell.

There was a space of time during which Miss Rachel lived in a disembodied condition on the outer fringes of consciousness. Then she came to herself and lay quiet, but awake. After a while she was able to make out the window, a lighter square in the blackness, and the white patch of counterpane on the bed. There was a feeling of air coming in at the door. She was alone.

When she first tried to stand up her head seemed obstinately to want to float in the air above her body. It was difficult to find the door, shut it, locate the light switch, and turn it on. The glare made her eyes swim with pain. It was then she saw the inkwell on the floor, knew that she had interrupted a prowler more acute than herself. With a singleness of purpose that belied her addled brain she went to Mrs. Karov's closet and looked through the garments hanging there. There were three house dresses, an old dark blue street dress, two hats, and several sweaters. But no coat.

Miss Rachel went and sat on Mrs. Karov's bed and rubbed her temples hard. She had now to get out of the Tellingham house without being found out and over to spend the night with the Hayeses, if it weren't too late. She had no idea of how long she might have lain unconscious on the floor. She wondered, too, what that other prowler had been about when she had interrupted him. Had the murderer, too, some interest in Mrs. Karov's clothes?

If there had been time she would have stayed and gone through the dresser drawers in an attempt to find what, if anything, could have attracted the other intruder. But since the chance to stay with the Hayeses was one not likely to come again, she let the search go. Still trembling, still with that aching feeling of headlessness, she turned off the lights and went out into the hall.

It was dark, but strips of light showed from under Mrs. Tellingham's door and Alma's. From Mrs. Tellingham's room came a subdued sound of crying. This gave Miss Rachel hope that she hadn't been out so long after all, that she could still reach the Hayes house without anything being amiss.

She hurried down the stairs, out into the night. Her own lights burned across the alley. Once in her own house, she gathered what she would need for a night's stay next door, darkened the house, and locked it, went by way of an opening in the hedge to the Hayes kitchen door.

Mrs. Hayes came in answer to her knock and said briskly but without much warmth: "Oh, so you *did* come after all. We're just sitting down to dinner. I hope you haven't had yours yet."

Miss Rachel squeezed past Mrs. Hayes's great bulk and into the kitchen. "Thanks. I would take a bite, if you have plenty."

"Always plenty, though I haven't done much fancy cooking since the tragedy about Mother." Under the bright light Mrs. Hayes showed traces of haggardness. When she reached for Miss Rachel's small package of night things her hand shook, though she made an obvious effort to control it. During the afternoon, since Mrs. Karov's murder, something had been working under that military calm. "Just go right in. Bill's waiting. I'll put your things upstairs and be right down." She walked off toward a small stairway that led up from the farther side of the kitchen.

Miss Rachel went through a pantry into a dining room, where Mr. Hayes wriggled up out of his chair to place one for Miss Rachel.

"Good evening. Glad you can be with us. House next door—dreadful stuff—you couldn't stay there." And yet he, too, seemed singularly unglad about Miss Rachel's presence. It was just as though—Miss Rachel tried to put the feeling into words—it was as though she were a necessary evil.

Miss Rachel sat down, and when Mr. Hayes joined them they proceeded to eat a plain but substantial meal.

There was only one time that things became a little awkward. That was when Mr. Hayes said suddenly in the middle of a conversation about the weather: "You look a little peaked, Miss Murdock. Did you have a fall or something? I notice your face seems swollen."

Miss Rachel felt impaled under their glance. She had pulled her white hair down a bit, covering the dark lump where the inkwell had struck her. Mr. Hayes's look might have been mildly inquiring or there might (and there seemed to be) a touch of malice behind it. Mrs. Hayes was perfectly inscrutable.

"Miss Rachel has gone through some trying experiences," she said to her husband. "Anyone might seem peaked, knowing that there was a murderer under their roof."

Mr. Hayes quit looking at Miss Rachel and stared at his wife. There was something unspoken in the fixity of his eyes, but Mrs. Hayes matched it. Miss Rachel recalled the situation between these two people earlier in the afternoon: Mrs. Hayes's assertion that her husband had gone out by the back, his angry denial that he had gone out at all. Things had not progressed since then; there had been no thrashing out of the question. Instead, it smoldered, and the smoke was getting in Mr. Hayes's eyes.

"Having a murderer under one's roof is a matter of opinion," he said carefully. "Some folks see murderers where none exist. Some people identify innocent members of their own families as murderers. Even"—he fairly bit the word—"even to the police."

Mrs. Hayes let her glance flit to Miss Rachel. Her hand, poised to take up the water glass, trembled ever so slightly.

"It's warm tonight, isn't it?" Her lip-cracking smile was a mask for a very unpleasant set of thoughts. "Warm for September."

Miss Rachel saw that she was one of several things: she was either a witness to the obvious fact that Mrs. Hayes thought Mr. Hayes was a murderer, or she was an audience before which they were putting on a little play for purposes of their own, or she was a brake to keep them from killing each other.

"This custard is very good," Miss Rachel said mildly. The conversation went on like that, with joints in it.

After the meal was cleared, the dishes done, and a few minutes spent listening to the news broadcast on the radio concerning mass murder instead of murder done singly, Mrs. Hayes made the suggestion that they all go to bed. It was a little after nine.

Miss Rachel followed Mrs. Hayes's majestic back up the front stairs to the upper bedrooms.

"We have an extra bedroom, but it's not very comfortable," Mrs. Hayes said, stopping in the hall. "I'm sure you'll be more comfortable in my room. Mr. Hayes will sleep across in the guest room."

"Oh, won't that be quite inconvenient?" Miss Rachel asked, disliking the idea of sleeping with Mrs. Hayes.

"Not at all. In fact, he suggested it." She led the way into a big room in which, to her relief, Miss Rachel saw twin beds. Her own night things were laid out on the one toward the windows. Mrs. Hayes shut the door carefully and locked it. "I always do that," she explained. "Couldn't sleep unless the door were locked." But Miss Rachel saw that the key was new, the lock old. Locking the door had involved getting a new key; the old one was most likely long misplaced.

It suddenly came over Miss Rachel that she didn't at all like being locked in with Mrs. Hayes. When the invitation to stay the night had first been given she had pictured herself as being alone, free to prowl the house if anything sounded suspicious.

Mrs. Hayes shed her clothes with military thoroughness. In the throes of getting out of her corset she stopped to ask: "Have the newspapermen bothered you much, Miss Murdock?"

"They're more interested in the lieutenant. He's official," Miss Rachel explained. "Though I did have my picture taken."

"What did the lieutenant tell them?"

"I don't know. As little as possible, I imagine. Sometimes valuable clues are made worthless through publicity."

Mrs. Hayes bit at a knot in her corset string, worried it with her teeth. "Such as?" she said indistinctly.

"Oh, I can't think of anything in particular." Miss Rachel tried definitely not to think of a number of things.

"What about Mrs. Karov? Were there many clues about her murder?"

"I suppose." Miss Rachel let her nightgown slide down over her underthings, undressed as if inside a tent. "There are always a *few*—"

"Shhhhh!" Mrs. Hayes was staring toward the door, the knob now slowly revolving. "Who is it?" she demanded loudly.

"Me!" said Mr. Hayes's voice. "I want my pajamas. And my slippers."

"Just a minute." Mrs. Hayes ran to the closet, dug out the

slippers, and took a pair of pajamas off the hook, ran back to the door and unlocked it with an air of caution.

"Judith, couldn't I *just*—" Mr. Hayes pleaded.

Mrs. Hayes wasn't majestic in a corset, pink bloomers, and hose, but Mr. Hayes couldn't see that, of course. "No, you can't," she flung through the crack.

What was it Mr. Hayes wanted? Miss Rachel wondered. Could it be a goodnight kiss? But when Mrs. Hayes relocked the door she was perspiring. Evidently to deny Mr. Hayes had taken some effort.

"Now," she said briskly, getting back to the knots, "you were going to tell me all about the clues they found with Mrs. Karov."

Miss Rachel didn't recall any such promise, but then Mayhew had shown the coat to the Tellinghams, and it wasn't a secret. Perhaps telling Mrs. Hayes about it would help along the solution of the mystery. Somehow there *had* to be more to that coat than there seemed to be!

"Well, the main thing was that coat. The one they found with her. It was a very dark blue, tailored, buttoned like a man's coat, and the Tellinghams thought that Mrs. Karov got it at a rummage sale."

Mrs. Hayes went on digging at knots. "How do they figure it's a clue if it belonged to the woman who was killed?"

"Well . . ." Miss Rachel's thoughts skittered across thin ice. "The main thing is that Mrs. Karov was under it and it was over her." This was weak and repetitious, but it gave her a chance to study Mrs. Hayes's reaction.

Mrs. Hayes looked no more than mildly interested. "Was that all there was?"

"The—the butcher knife."

Mrs. Hayes looked hard at her. "It was mine."

"Oh, of course, but, you see, even the fact of its being there must mean something."

Mrs. Hayes stared significantly at the door. "I agree with you there."

"And then there were"—Miss Rachel took a deep breath and plunged—"there were the letters."

Mrs. Hayes actually looked startled. "The letters to Ronald Byers? Did they find them?"

"Yes, and Lieutenant Mayhew took them away."

"Did Ronald get to read them?"

"I think so."

Mrs. Hayes seemed to go off into deep thought. Slowly, meditatively, she emerged from her corset and put on a gown. In the long straight cotton garment she looked majestic again, like some gigantic priestess full of contemplation. "They'll get married now," she said after a while. "And the whole thing will come to a dead end."

She made no further explanation. Ten minutes after the lights were out she began gently to snore.

Miss Rachel slept in fits and starts. For quite a while there was an occasional sound from across the hall, where Mr. Hayes was unaccustomedly alone, and through the window drifted a trace of traffic noises from the downtown boulevards. But for the rest, there was quiet. Too much quiet.

It must have been nearly midnight when Mrs. Hayes got out of bed and bent over Miss Rachel. Miss Rachel happened to be awake, but she had presence of mind enough to keep breathing steadily and to remain relaxed. With a sigh Mrs. Hayes straightened up and went toward the closet. She must have had a very small flashlight, for it made a spot of light not much bigger than a nickel as it traveled over Miss Rachel's clothes.

The door squeaked a little as Mrs. Hayes unlocked it. Miss Rachel, watching from the bed, saw that she stood a long while listening before she went through. With no more sound than a ghost Miss Rachel went after her.

She was in the guest room now, the spot of light traveling rapidly over Mr. Hayes's baggy pants and unpressed coat where they lay across a chair. Mr. Hayes's snores were a little more emphatic than his wife's. Occasionally be rumbled. When he did, the light went off and Mrs. Hayes waited, quite silently, in the dark.

Miss Rachel darted back into bed as the woman started to leave, but a few moments of rigid listening convinced her that Mrs. Hayes was going downstairs.

Miss Rachel flew after, almost fell down the stairs, then realized that Mrs. Hayes had gone by the back way into the kitchen.

Miss Rachel peeped from the kitchen staircase to find Mrs. Hayes standing at the door, which, like Miss Rachel's, had a pane in its upper half. There was no way of telling what Mrs. Hayes saw out there in the back yard. Indeed, from what little Miss Rachel could make out of her, she seemed to be not so much looking as listening.

She left the kitchen door after a few minutes and walked slowly down the short passage to a door which led off from the dining room. Miss Rachel remembered the woman's testimony to Mayhew, that Mrs. Ruddick had had a room downstairs and at the opposite side of the house from the Hayeses. This room she was entering fitted that description. Miss Rachel, not without palpitations, followed until she could see in through the door. Mrs. Hayes's little light, like a firefly, made spiralings of yellow. Then there was the sound of shades being drawn, and the overhead bulb flashed on.

Miss Rachel had a hunch that she had better get out, and yet she was impelled to see what Mrs. Hayes might be up to.

Mrs. Hayes first ran rapidly through the contents of Mrs. Ruddick's dresser. There was a fixed look in her eye, as though she knew exactly what she wanted. When the dresser proved barren she took a chair into the closet, and Miss Rachel heard the creak of the chair and the bump of something heavy hitting the floor.

Mrs. Hayes emerged from the closet with a box which she put on the bed and began to unpack. It contained—to Miss Rachel's surprise and disappointment—a great many books.

Somewhere near the bottom Mrs. Hayes found a snapshot album. Off it she blew a great deal of dust and then sat down with it and ruffled the pages. At about the halfway mark she paused and stared so long and so intently at one page that Miss Rachel wondered if she might not be falling asleep.

There was no expression of satisfaction or even of much interest on Mrs. Hayes's face. She simply looked and absorbed whatever it was she had found, and after a long while she made preparations to go. These involved packing up the box—except the album—putting it away and replacing the chair. The lights went out, the shades up. But by then Miss Rachel was halfway upstairs.

When Mrs. Hayes came back into the bedroom she first put the album into the one place, in Miss Rachel's opinion, where anyone would look for it: under her mattress. Then she came and again bent over Miss Rachel. Miss Rachel lay very still and breathed like a baby.

But there was more to it this time. Mrs. Hayes's hands sought out and found Miss Rachel's form; for an instant the small elderly lady had visions of being strangled. Then Mrs. Hayes began shaking her.

"Wake up, Miss Murdock." *Shake, shake.* "Wake up, but don't make any noise."

Miss Rachel put on as good an imitation as she was capable of, considering that she had never watched herself wake up. "Uh? Oh. Who is it? What do you want? Is it you, Mrs. Hayes?"

"Shhhhh!" Mrs. Hayes hissed like a snake, then put her lips to Miss Rachel's ear. "There's something I want you to know so that you can tell Lieutenant Mayhew."

Miss Rachel dropped all pretense. "Yes? What is it?"

"I can tell you," Mrs. Hayes promised in a hoarse whisper, "where Mrs. Karov got that *coat!*"

CHAPTER FIFTEEN

MISS RACHEL sat up and stared through the dark to where Mrs. Hayes's face shone like a dim moon. "Where? Where did she get it?" The moon withdrew a little before her eagerness.

"She got it out of a box put out for a Salvation Army collector, right in this neighborhood. When she thought nobody was looking, of course."

"How long ago?" Miss Rachel demanded breathlessly.

"Eight years or so. It happened while Annie and Ronald were living next door—that's how I came to notice. When you mentioned the coat tonight it roused something in my memory; I've been thinking ever since. I'm sure that Annie put it out in a box on the porch. It had belonged to Ronald; I think he wore it from the time he was about sixteen till he was grown."

Miss Rachel groped for the light switch and clicked it on, hurried to the closet, and began to get into her clothes any which way.

"What are you going to do?" Mrs. Hayes asked as if in surprise.

"I'm dressing," Miss Rachel said unnecessarily.

Mrs. Hayes sat and watched; whether it was an unexpected development, Miss Rachel had no way of knowing. She looked much as she had when staring into the album: contemplative, disinterested.

"I suppose I should have waited till morning to tell you."

"Not in this case you shouldn't," Miss Rachel told her.

"After all," Mrs. Hayes ruminated, "the coat isn't so terribly important. It's just that I remembered where Mrs. Karov must have gotten it, and I thought the lieutenant might be interested."

"You've no idea how interested he's going to be." Miss Rachel finished lacing her low Oxfords. "Now I wish to use your telephone. And by the way—could you prove that the coat belonged to Ronald Byers if he should deny it?"

A gleam of satisfaction, quickly suppressed, shone in Mrs. Hayes's eye. Miss Rachel had a momentary glimpse into the woman's heart, and she saw there Mrs. Hayes's old resentment, well covered these many years, over the treatment Ronald had given Annie and her deep desire to involve the man in the crime of killing Mrs. Karov.

"I think I could prove it well enough. You see, there's a picture"—her glance flickered toward the mattress—"and it shows Ronald with Annie and Alma and Bernice, all of them down at the beach. And there is Ronald's coat, as big as you please, hung over a bench. Anybody with two eyes can see it's the same coat."

"Thank you." Miss Rachel made for the door.

Mrs. Hayes did not follow her down into the lower hall, but Miss Rachel felt her presence hanging over the upper banisters, listening.

Lieutenant Mayhew sounded drowsy but interested. Miss Rachel explained the point about the coat. "You'd better bring it out tonight and ask Ronald Byers about it."

"I don't see your reasons for the hurry." Mayhew paused to stifle a yawn. "What if Mrs. Karov did pick it out of a box on

Ronald Byers' porch? It still doesn't make her anything but a ragpicker. A good one at that." Mayhew evidently appreciated the fine points of the coat.

"Please bring that coat out here. It's important. It's got to be identified."

"I'll be out in the morning."

Miss Rachel had reached the point of desperation. Her hands on the receiver were clammy; her breath stuck in her throat. "Look, I'm going to have to admit that I haven't been exactly honest about everything. There was something, something that happened that night the prowler was on the roof of my porch. It—it—" This was getting difficult. She could feel a stiffness coming over the wire, as though Mayhew were going to be very angry. "I'll tell you about it when I see you."

"I'll be right out," Mayhew said crisply.

"And bring the coat," Miss Rachel reminded.

"Don't worry."

He *was* going to be angry!

Twenty minutes later she was sure of it. On the Hayes front porch Mayhew loomed big and brown and very official. Miss Rachel wondered how long it had been since he remembered she had brought him Sara. Quite a while, she imagined. When he was thinking of Sara he didn't frown and his mouth didn't make a straight line in his face as though a tired sculptor had put it in with a single stroke of a chisel. And that's the way he looked now.

Miss Rachel got out of the door before Mrs. Hayes could put a word in. "We'd better go next door to talk. If you've brought the coat. . . ."

"I brought it."

He followed, his feet making a hollow sound on the brick

walk. The night was brisk, the sky like a black cake full of big yellow candles. Miss Rachel unlocked the front door, let him go in before her. In the living room she turned on lights and motioned for him to sit down. He had a newspaper-wrapped bulky bundle which he set at his feet—evidently the coat which had covered dead Mrs. Karov.

"I believe you said you have some evidence which I don't know about," he began, getting right to the point.

"Yes, I—I have. I didn't mean deliberately to conceal it."

Oh, didn't you? said Miss Rachel's conscience.

She lifted the hem of her petticoat, ran her fingers about on the underside; looking for the button. "I couldn't quite make up my mind whether it was important or not. You see, when that person on the roof climbed down my trellis he lost a button. It was a dark blue coat button with an oak-leaf design in the middle and a milled border." Mayhew was beginning to be interested; one hand strayed toward the strings of the bundle at his feet. "And as soon as I saw that coat on Mrs. Karov I recognized the design. My button, the one I got off the trellis, was a duplicate of those on the coat. Only, you see, *there weren't any missing!*"

Odd that she should forget where she had sewn the button! She could have sworn it was here on the left side. Mayhew watched as she lifted the right hem, modestly explored its inner surface.

He broke the strings on the bundle and took out Mrs. Karov's coat and shook it out. Buttons gleamed down its front and on its belt.

"Just what," he asked mildly, "gave you the idea that that other button wasn't important?"

Her fingers raced, her mind puzzled with the problem of her

own forgetfulness. "It's gone," she said stupidly. Her fingers had found a nubbin of torn thread. "It's been pulled off."

Mayhew looked unbelieving, and that gave Miss Rachel the courage to do what she next did, to march back through the dark to Mrs. Hayes, who was sitting in her lighted living room pretending to look at a magazine. "Yes?" said Mrs. Hayes at the door.

Miss Rachel put out her hand. "The button!" she said with the air of a conspirator.

"Button? What button?" cried Mrs. Hayes, but she was trying to think fast, faster than Miss Rachel.

"Tonight, when you thought your husband and I asleep, you searched our clothing, perhaps in the hope of finding bloodstains and so solving the murder of your mother." Mrs. Hayes, at this, tried to look like a detective. "In the hem of my petticoat," Miss Rachel continued, "you must have found a button. You took it for evidence." This was putting a good face on it. Miss Rachel now thrust her palm under Mrs. Hayes's nose. "I want it." She stepped aside a few inches, enough to show Mayhew coming up the steps of the porch. "You see," she hissed, "it connects Ronald's coat with the murderer."

Mrs. Hayes reached promptly into the pocket of her kimono; her eyes fairly glistened, and into Miss Rachel's hand fell a bit of blue plastic.

Mayhew stared over Miss Rachel's shoulder and then put out a hand for the evidence.

"And now," Miss Rachel said, looking wise, "the picture!"

For an instant she thought Mrs. Hayes was about to balk, and then the big woman turned and, leaving the door open, proceeded upstairs. When she returned she carried the album with a thumb stuck into its middle pages.

"This is it." The pages fell apart, and Miss Rachel found herself looking at a group of people on a beach, garbed in the style of the '20s. "Here's Ronald. This is Bernice, hogging the foreground. Back here is Alma and Annie."

Annie was a child in pigtails. Bernice and Ronald and Alma were well up into their teens. In the far background, about a tablecloth spread on the sand, Miss Rachel found a youthful Mr. and Mrs. Hayes, a young and lovely Mrs. Tellingham, a middle-aged but not unhandsome elder Mr. Byers, and an old lady whom she didn't recognize.

"Mother wasn't with us that day," Mrs. Hayes said, explaining the absence of Mrs. Ruddick. "This one"—she pointed out the old lady—"that's Alma's grandmother, Barbara Tellingham. The old—" Her voice died on the epithet as Mayhew glanced at her. "Anyway," she concluded with an air of finality, "that's all of it. There's your proof that Ronald owned that coat."

It was true. Beside Ronald was a mass of dark material thrown over a bench. The cut, the arrangement of buttons, the look of the garment, were unmistakable. Miss Rachel held the album toward the light. For an instant she thought of saying something about the bulk of the thing—in the picture there might have been two coats there together—and then decided not to spoil things. After all, she did have Mayhew interested at last.

Mayhew took the coat and the album to Miss Rachel's house and left her there with them and then disappeared in the dark in the direction of the Byers house.

He came back in about ten minutes, and Ronald Byers was with him. Mayhew showed him the coat.

Ronald fingered the buttons, spread the shoulders, and examined the pockets. "This was mine, all right. Here"—he indicated a torn pocket corner—"here's where I used to carry a thermos bottle to work when I was about eighteen and worked part time in a grocery."

"And you haven't any idea of how Mrs. Karov came into possession of it?"

Ronald shook his head. "None whatever. I haven't seen the thing for years. In fact, I didn't really know what had become of it."

"Try to think when you did actually last see it," Mayhew suggested.

Ronald let go the coat and stared at the black panes of the windows. "Alma and I must have been about twenty-one when we went to Arrowhead, and she needed an extra coat and I brought this one. I remember her sitting by the campfire in it. There was quite a bunch of us, and I had a hard time finding her. Her hair's dark, and the dark coat . . . She laughed when I finally found her."

He glanced at Mayhew, and Miss Rachel held her breath.

Dark coat . . . dark hair . . . he'd hardly been able to find her. Did he have any idea of what he was saying?

"I see." Mayhew folded the coat and let it down into its nest of wrappings. "You don't recall your wife's saying that she meant to put it out for a charity collection?"

"Of course you do!" The voice belonged to Bernice, who had come in with out any sound and now stood in the doorway. "Annie put that coat out for the Salvation Army. Don't you remember?"

Ronald shook his head. "I always connected the coat with Alma, somehow. You know, she liked it."

Through Miss Rachel's mind fled all that she knew about Alma, and especially the fact that Alma must have lied in saying that when she sat in her chair in her bedroom she could not see the rear of Miss Rachel's house.

"What about this coat?" Bernice asked, coming in. "Is it connected somehow with the murders?"

Mayhew explained very briefly about its having belonged to Mrs. Karov.

"But of course!" Bernice agreed. "She must have taken it out of the box before the collector came."

"I don't quite see," Ronald said carefully, "just what importance this thing has. Mrs. Karov might have taken it. So what?"

"Coats usually come with one or two extra buttons, sometimes in an envelope, sometimes on a loop of thread," Mayhew said. "I was wondering if this coat had had any such extra buttons, and if so, where they might be now."

Bernice and Ronald looked at each other blankly.

"I've always attended to the sewing. Mother died so many years ago," Bernice explained. "And I don't remember any extra buttons, ever. Though I could, of course, look in my button box."

"Would you do that?" Mayhew asked.

She looked at him uncertainly. "Do you mean right away?"

"If you don't mind."

"Of course not." She had turned from the living-room doorway, wrapping her blue crepe negligee lightly about her, as if to face the night. Even in pale blue, with the hem of a chiffon gown showing beneath, Bernice looked like nothing but a spinster.

Miss Rachel followed her quickly to the front entry. "Could I come too? I've become so interested in all this. It's gruesome and yet so fascinating." Miss Rachel put on an expression of what she hoped was simpering innocence.

Bernice Byers looked at her with ill-concealed impatience.

"You may come along, of course. Though I'm afraid I can't promise much excitement."

They went out into the dark, and Miss Rachel hurried to keep up with the flowing blue robe ahead. The Byers house was well lighted, windows with lights behind them both upstairs and down. Bernice rapped at the door, and Grandpa admitted them. His white hair was a tousled halo under the overhead bulb.

"Good evening," he said formally to Miss Rachel and watched as they hurried past to the stairs.

Bernice's bedroom was a contradictory affair. On the walls was a mixture of school trophies—badges and certificates won in tennis and other sports—and some very good etchings which indicated an adult taste. On the dresser was a picture of herself and Ronald, almost identical at about the age of five or six—Ronald identifiable only by the absence of a hair ribbon.

On the bed were two dolls, one a Raggedy Ann of childhood days, the other a sophisticated French lady with a leering expression. The whole room was a contrast between the showiness and self-importance of a child and the more subdued personality of a woman. And the eyes of the little Bernice in the picture, her sweatered arm possessively through Ronald's, were somehow the same as the eyes which looked at Miss Rachel now from across the button box.

In this latter there were big and little buttons, round and square and odd-shaped buttons, pink and blue and red and black buttons. But no buttons to match the coat that had belonged to Mrs. Karov.

Bernice, in the end, let Miss Rachel look for herself.

Miss Rachel went back to Mayhew full of disappointment. She had banked heavily on the clue of the button, and she had lost. The coat had been Ronald's and then had belonged to Mrs. Karov, and Mrs. Karov had worn it to her death. And nowhere—though it should, she knew, *it should*—did the button from the trellis fit in at all.

Bernice, after reporting to Mayhew that she had not been able to find any duplicate buttons in her box, went home and took Ronald with her. And Mayhew wrapped up the coat and advised Miss Rachel to go to bed. Elsewhere, preferably.

"I couldn't sleep," she told him. "Not if my life depended on it. I want to think."

He left her unwillingly. Miss Rachel brewed a pot of tea and sat down by the radio in the living room and tuned in an all-night program. At first she had to endure much swing music and a great many commercials, but as the night waned the program changed to organ music. It must have been three-thirty or four when Miss Rachel dropped off to sleep, sitting cramped in her chair, the teacup balanced on its arm, the organ spinning a web of dreams in her head.

She wakened abruptly when the teacup fell. Her sleepy eyes opened on the garish room, the carpetless floor, the rickety furniture, and for an instant she wondered where on earth she might be.

Then, seeing the figure that stood watching from the door, she knew.

CHAPTER SIXTEEN

MRS. TELLINGHAM advanced as though she were walking in her sleep. The half-tied cord at the waist of the yellow robe, the absence of slippers, the surf of gray hair that shadowed her eyes, betrayed hurry and agitation. She put out a hand; the rigid fingers were white. "Alma!" she said. Then she sneezed.

Miss Rachel stood up with difficulty. Spots of her were numb all over her body. "Mrs. Tellingham! Are you awake?"

"Of course!" She choked back another sneeze. "Why do you think I'm not awake? I've never been asleep." Her gaze raked the walls, the black panes of the windows. "I'm looking for Alma. She's gone."

A shiver started at the base of Miss Rachel's spine and worked its way up. "How long has it been since you saw her?"

"Tonight, when she went to her room." One of Mrs. Tellingham's distracted hands started to retie the cord at her waist. "I've got to find her. I can't let her be lost."

"What makes you think she'd be here?"

"Where else would she be? She wouldn't go to the Hayeses'. Ronald couldn't take her in." The befogged eyes sought Miss Rachel's approval of this logic. "Look for her, won't you?"

Miss Rachel looked, from the upper bedrooms down to the

pantry. Mrs. Tellingham followed her in the search, stood behind her as Miss Rachel looked down into the blackness of the cellar.

"You stay here," Miss Rachel decided. She took matches from the kitchen to light her way. The cellar smelled of dampness, of old ashes, of dust and, standing in the middle of the floor in a little island of yellow light, Miss Rachel felt her skin creep. If Alma were down here . . . She went slowly to the closet. It was empty. The space behind the furnace was bare likewise.

Mrs. Tellingham seemed to float at the stairhead like a yellow wraith. "Did you find her?"

"No," Miss Rachel said in relief.

"Will you come back with me and look in my house?"

Impatience stirred in Miss Rachel; if Alma Tellingham were gone Mayhew should know it, and immediately. A prolonged search was silly and dangerous. "Will you?" said Mrs. Tellingham. There was a quivering overtone to her voice. Miss Rachel went up and in the pantry, for one instant, she found Mrs. Tellingham's eyes free of the pretense of puzzlement. She hadn't realized that Miss Rachel was watching, or else the strain was momentarily too much. The blankness washed away, and stark ravening terror took its place.

"What's wrong?" Miss Rachel asked quickly.

"Just—just that Alma's angry with me and she's gone." Mrs. Tellingham had turned to the kitchen door. "You will help me find her, won't you?" She had reached the black pane that faced the back yard. But when Miss Rachel approached she let her go first.

In the Tellingham house Miss Rachel repeated the process of trying to find Alma, and with the same result. Mrs. Tellingham dragged the search out to a tedious length, thinking up new cubbyholes at intervals, until at last Miss Rachel took things into her own hands and sat down at the telephone.

While they waited for Mayhew, Miss Rachel decided to do a bit of investigating on her own. Mrs. Tellingham still persisted in following with an over-the-shoulder expression in the depths of her eyes, and that was a nuisance, but there was no help for it.

Miss Rachel went up to Mrs. Karov's room and searched it thoroughly, looking for she knew not what—until she found it. Under a pile of black cotton stockings in the second bureau drawer was a coarse loop of thread with three buttons on it. Blue buttons with an oak-leaf design and a milled border. Miss Rachel stood and looked, then dangled them in Mrs. Tellingham's direction.

Mrs. Tellingham tore her gaze from the open doorway long enough to see what it was Miss Rachel had.

"Do you remember seeing these buttons in Mrs. Karov's belongings?"

"It must be a European custom to keep so many odds and ends of things," Mrs. Tellingham said inconclusively. "But I don't recall them, no."

"Had you looked through her stuff since she died?"

"Oh, a little. Alma packed a few of her things to send to New York. That's where her uncle, or someone, lives."

"Do you place these?"

Mrs. Tellingham stared at the window, where the curtains moved slowly on an early-morning breeze. She swallowed. "Isn't there something out there, outside the window?"

Miss Rachel switched off the lights and ran to the pane. But out of doors, where the dawn was coming up in green and silver, was nothing—not even a porch roof, as in the case of her own intruder.

"There isn't anything," she told Mrs. Tellingham, who had gone to the bed and sat down.

Mrs. Tellingham continued to shake and stare, taking Miss Rachel's impatient attention off the string of buttons.

"Do you know, I saw something tonight that I—I wouldn't have believed a month ago. It must be the effect of these murders, the things that have come out about Mother's will, and all." She put the heels of her hands to her temples, and the tendons stood out in her wrists as she pressed. "I'm either going mad or—or the dead can come back and haunt the living."

Miss Rachel, the buttons in her palm, sat at the opposite end of the bed and watched Mrs. Tellingham. "What do you think you saw?"

Mrs. Tellingham seemed to listen a moment before she answered. "I saw Mrs. Karov," she said finally. "That's impossible."

"I know."

There was a minute of silence, during which Mrs. Tellingham's breath took on an asthmatic hoarseness and all of the blood washed out of her face as if she were being drained. "I know it's quite impossible. And yet that—that's what I saw."

"Where?"

"In this house. In the hall. Not far from the door to this room. It was just a flash, and yet there wasn't any mistaking it."

"You saw her face to face?" asked Miss Rachel, anxious to probe the depths of the hallucination.

"She was just going downstairs, very slowly, not making any sound. I was on my way to Alma's room; I'd got out into the hall before I noticed this—*it*—and then I must have nearly fainted, for it was a moment or so before I felt myself again. And it was gone."

"Was that when you missed Alma?" Miss Rachel asked thoughtfully.

"Yes. I went on into Alma's room. I felt sick and stupid and all hollow inside. And she wasn't there."

"Then what did you do?"

"I made myself look for her, though I had a terrible fear of seeing the thing again. And when I couldn't find Alma in the house I had to see someone, some other human being, somebody alive." She shuddered all over; the act reminded Miss Rachel of a policeman's stallion she had once seen, forced to submit to being tied to a dead dray horse and to pull it off the street. There was the same ripple under the flesh, looseness of bone, look of uncomprehending horror. "So I went over to you."

Miss Rachel took her by the hand and led her out of the room. "I want you to stand just where you stood when you saw this thing. And then I'll start down the stairs, and you stop me when I'm where it was."

Miss Rachel started down, looking back at Mrs. Tellingham.

Mrs. Tellingham opened her mouth when Miss Rachel was at the fourth step; her lips formed the word *there*, but no sound came out.

"Would you take me for Mrs. Karov?"

Mrs. Tellingham shook her head. "You aren't *dressed* like Mrs. Karov!"

Miss Rachel faced about, and from below the doorbell shrilled. Mayhew had come; there was no time for further questions now.

"That will be Lieutenant Mayhew. You'd better come down and tell him about Alma. Try to think of any friends she might have gone to for the night."

Mrs. Tellingham began to tidy her hair. Her bare feet for the first time seemed to attract her attention. "I'll get some slippers from my room. Go down and let him in, won't you?"

When Mrs. Tellingham joined Mayhew and Miss Rachel in the living room there was a veneer of control on her. Her jaw line was hard, but it was a hysterical hardness and apt to crack. Mayhew had been listening to Miss Rachel's theories about the buttons. When Mrs. Tellingham came in he stood up and, as if to give her immediate relief for her feelings, asked for the details of Alma's disappearance.

"Sit down." Mrs. Tellingham took a chair just out of range of the floor lamp. "I don't want to bore you by sounding like an overwrought, imaginative mother. But Alma's never done this before and—and there was a very unpleasant thing happened just before I discovered she was gone."

"Miss Murdock has told me about the figure you saw." Mayhew tried to fix Mrs. Tellingham's haunted eyes with his own. "Now I want you to think very carefully. Could this figure you saw going downstairs have been your daughter?"

"No," Mrs. Tellingham said quickly. And then less quickly: "I don't see how it could have been."

"Do you mean the shape of the body, the size, and so forth?"

She tied and untied the cord at her waist before answering. "It just wasn't Alma. It couldn't have been."

Mayhew swung off on another tack. "Could you give me some idea of where your daughter may have gone, some friend's house where she'd be sure of being welcome?"

Mrs. Tellingham, after considerable thought, offered two names which Mayhew proceeded to look up in the telephone directory and call. Both were the numbers of women with whom Alma had been friends at school. But Alma was with neither.

Mayhew then made a few calls on his own: to headquarters, with instructions for squad cars in this end of town to keep an eye out for a young woman answering Alma's description—Mrs. Tellingham meanwhile having gone upstairs to discover what clothes she might be wearing—and to various bus and train depots.

She wouldn't leave Los Angeles," Mrs. Tellingham protested. "She'd have taken a bag and extra clothes."

"This is routine," Mayhew assured her. "And now, would you mind if I had a look through your daughter's room?"

Mrs. Tellingham looked at him indifferently. "I don't mind, if it will help you to find her."

Mayhew went upstairs, and Mrs. Tellingham stayed with Miss Rachel. The over-the-shoulder expression was back. "I don't feel very well. Not like—like staying alone, I mean. I was wondering"—she bit her lips, stared at her clenched hands—"could you perhaps spend a while with me?"

"I'll be glad to stay until you have definite news of your daughter," Miss Rachel promised. "Perhaps, meanwhile, you'd better lie down. You must be exhausted."

"Oh, I couldn't sleep." She got out of her chair and began to pace the length of the windows. Outside the increased light was pouring color into the lawn and the shrubbery, and the birds had begun to come down to look for breakfast. "I couldn't risk shutting my eyes and waking up to see *it*."

The truth, Miss Rachel saw, was that Mrs. Tellingham had come to her in the night, had allowed Mayhew to be called, and had asked for further companionship not because of her loss of Alma or any worry over where the girl might be, but because she was afraid of *a ghost!*

"I'm so wide awake myself," Miss Rachel offered, "that I'd be glad to sit in your room if you would try to rest. There wouldn't be any danger of my dropping off to sleep. And I'm sure that you wouldn't see the thing that frightened you again." *Not without my seeing it too*, she added mentally. Miss Rachel was beginning to have ideas about that figure.

Mrs. Tellingham, with the light coming in over her head, looked like some shadowy corpse herself. "Would you? It's asking a lot. . . ."

"Let's go up now," Miss Rachel suggested.

On her bed, Mrs. Tellingham looked thin and flat, as though she had receded to two dimensions like a paper doll. Miss Rachel covered her with a taffeta comforter, went to the other side of the room, and sat down. Mrs. Tellingham's big eyes regarded her from the pillow. Occasionally the sounds made by Mayhew in his rummaging came through the walls. For the rest there was silence.

"How was it," Mrs. Tellingham said in a half whisper, "you came here just as all these dreadful things started to happen?"

Miss Rachel's thought flew back to that first afternoon, to Claudia and the toad, the watchful Mrs. Karov, the atmosphere of ready-to-burst malignancy. "I don't know," she answered, deciding against trying to explain all of this. "I suppose it was what the Hindus call *Kismet*."

"Fate?" Mrs. Tellingham let out a long breath, her first sign of relaxation. "I suppose it was fate, too, that took Mrs. Ruddick into the cellar."

"Not at all. Mrs. Ruddick wanted her letters, the ones she had taken from Ronald before he could read them. The ones Alma wrote. They'd been stolen from Mrs. Ruddick, you see, and she wanted them back." And Miss Rachel's thought stumbled here over the old problem: *who* had taken the letters from Mrs. Ruddick and hidden them?

The Hayeses? Either of them, Miss Rachel thought, might have done it. Neither would have been anxious to reconcile the man and the girl who had wronged Annie. Suppose Mrs. Ruddick had found the hidden letters, accused one of them in anger, perhaps threatened to change her will. That would have done it, given the accused a perfect motive for killing her. Then killing Mrs. Karov would have followed to prevent identification and to continue the separation of Ronald and Alma by keeping the letters (which Mrs. Karov had located) from coming to light.

That was the case against the Hayeses. What about the Byerses?

Ronald's motives and opportunities she had previously analyzed. What of Grandpa? If he had stolen the letters from Mrs. Ruddick he, too, had a motive for not handing them over to Ronald. He disliked Alma. Murdering Mrs. Ruddick had also given him greater power in the committee which controlled the Tellingham property. He was now one of two, with an equal vote to Mrs. Tellingham's. As for Bernice, there was a lack of motive unless she had been acting for her father, which Miss Rachel couldn't quite imagine. It seemed, from what she had seen of the relations between the two, more apt to be the other way around.

Mrs. Tellingham was breathing deeply, and her eyes were shut. The breast of the robe cast a yellow reflection along her lips and into the hollows under her eyes. There was a puckery look to her chin, as though even in her sleep she was afraid and ready to cry.

Miss Rachel stepped across the hall to Alma's room, where Mayhew was carefully putting the last of Alma's writing material into a portfolio.

"Did you find anything?"

"Nothing to tell where she's gone." He took his hat off a chair. "If the police call here before I get downtown tell them to call me at headquarters. If they've located Alma Tellingham get her mother to talk to her."

"Why do you think she's run away?"

"I think she knows, or thinks she knows, who killed the two women in the cellar. Perhaps"—he shrugged resignedly—"she did it herself. In which case she's going to be harder to find."

Miss Rachel showed him the position of Alma's chair, from which she must have seen something of the murderer's entry into Miss Rachel's back door.

"That makes it look as though it might be Ronald Byers," Mayhew said. "She'd try to protect him because she loves him."

"You don't think that there's a possibility something might have happened to her?"

He looked past Miss Rachel to where the sun was stippling the curtains with light. "The thing has a pattern to it. It has to have. And there is a limited number of patterns. It could be that one of the Hayeses did the killing for the inheritance they'd get from the old lady, in which case there won't be apt to be any more murders, because the money is safely theirs. Or the other possibility—" A flicker of dissatisfaction came into his expression. "It's not pleasant to think about."

"What is it?" Miss Rachel asked because she had to know.

"Obviously, to get rid of the controls set up on the Tellingham property."

"You mean—?"

"Four of these people are in a race for survivorship. The old Mr. Byers, Alma, Alma's mother, and Claudia. The last man takes all."

"Claudia? But how—?"

There was a high scream from out of doors. Mayhew and Miss Rachel reached the window at the exact moment that Claudia's body, hurtling from the broken rope of her swing, flew over the rosebushes and crashed by the white stone that marked the grave of the toad.

CHAPTER SEVENTEEN

MISS RACHEL remembered afterward with a hideous clarity every step of the stairs, every door, every carpet and sill and impeding bit of furniture on her flight out to that broken figure under the rosebushes. If she breathed, she never knew it. From the time she saw Claudia flung head-on until she reached her was an agony of propulsion, of nightmare slowness under the drive of horror and fear. And then there was Claudia, at last, bloody and very still.

She tried to lift her, and Mayhew said, "Let me."

Miss Rachel hadn't heard him, didn't realize until now that his hurry must have matched her own. She saw his arms slide carefully under Claudia's knees and shoulders, and then Claudia's head fell aside with an odd dislocated movement. Miss Rachel screamed. She didn't ever remember screaming before, no matter what the stress. Mayhew looked at her sternly.

"You go ahead and open the door." He nodded toward Claudia's home. "Then get on the phone for the doctor."

Miss Rachel crushed her disorderly impulses and picked her skirts away from the rosebushes. They had reached the dividing line between the yards when Bernice stuck her head out at the back door and said, "Claudia! Breakfast's ready!"

Her eyes hesitated on Mayhew, fastened on the bundle he carried. "What's—? Is something wrong?" Then, since there was no mistaking what Mayhew carried, she came through the door and began running toward them. "Claudia! *Claudia!*"

She tried to snatch the child away, and Mayhew fended her off with a shoulder. "Let's move her as little as possible," he warned. "If you have a bed on the lower floor get it ready."

Miss Rachel was already inside. Grandpa was just coming into the kitchen. He looked shiny and alert—surprised when he saw Miss Rachel's hurry. "Something wrong again?" he asked.

She didn't wait to answer. In a moment she had the telephone, and Grandpa, still not understanding, supplied the doctor's telephone number from the doorway. That much arranged for, Miss Rachel followed Mayhew and Bernice into a room fitted up like a den or a study—Ronald's sanctum, most likely—where Claudia was put down gently upon a couch.

There followed a time of waiting which for Miss Rachel was hard to endure. Claudia's face, splotched with leafmold and soil, was a focal point around which everything else revolved. Bernice came up once with a wet cloth, but Mayhew, who had just come in again from the back yard, stopped her.

"Don't touch her face or her head. Even the weight of your hand inside that cloth could cause further brain injury if her skull is fractured."

Bernice drew her hand away, and though she accepted what Mayhew had said it seemed for an instant as though she were going to be sulky. She folded the cloth into a tight roll. "I've warned Claudia about jumping from the swing. I knew that someday she'd underestimate her distance. If children could just obey—"

"Claudia didn't jump," Miss Rachel cut in. "Her swing broke, and she was thrown."

"Her swing," Mayhew said noncommittally, "had been tampered with."

There was a funny silence on the part of Bernice and Grandpa. Bernice dropped the wet cloth, and one of Grandpa's hands went up aimlessly to stroke at his chin.

Mayhew had taken a short length of rope out of his pocket. "This was cut nearly through in two places under the board she sat on," he explained. He seemed to make no attempt to read the two faces turned toward him. "A small section is raveled where it tore apart. The rest was cut with a sharp knife."

No one said anything. Miss Rachel looked at Claudia, wondered what Claudia might tell them if she were able. Had she seen anyone at her swing this morning? When the doctor finally arrived and Mayhew had spoken to him for a moment in the hall, everyone was sent out of the room save Miss Rachel. What effect this would have on Bernice she could well imagine. The woman would be seething.

The doctor made a careful examination. "She can be moved," he decided.

Claudia was taken upstairs.

Ronald Byers stood in the crowd at the corner of Seventh and Broadway. The signal changed; the knot of people at the curb surged out toward the middle of the street. Ronald stared at the other corner, then abruptly drew back. A fat man ran into him, and there was a second or so of exasperated apology. Then Ronald had reached the window of the drugstore, stood before it with his back to the sidewalk. For nearly five minutes there were no further developments.

Mayhew had gone into the cigar store across the street. He

had to keep out of sight because his figure was well known to Byers, would attract his eye in a crowd, It would have been better for the sake of anonymity to have assigned another man to tail Byers, and yet the other man might not have recognized the person Byers had obviously intended to meet or have acted quickly enough when it was necessary.

As Byers stood there, his figure making a dark blotch in a window full of toothbrushes, his whole attitude betraying tension and nervousness, a girl slipped from the passing crowd to walk closely behind him. When she had gone a folded white paper lay at Byers' feet.

Mayhew's eye followed Alma Tellingham long enough to place her general direction, then switched back to Byers. To his surprise the other had made no move. The square of white lay at his heels, just as it had fallen; a shift of an inch would have brought him to stand on it. He stood there oblivious, unknowing.

Mayhew left the counter hurriedly, jostled through the crowd, and went across the intersection at a speed just under a lope. No one paid him any heed; all were too intent on their own destination. Just behind Byers he stooped and picked up the note.

Byers whirled; for an instant he was confused, and then far off he must have seen Alma's rapidly disappearing back. He reached for what Mayhew had, and Mayhew held it away. Byers' eyes blazed. He let fly an inaccurate left hook which Mayhew ducked.

He then attempted to straight-arm Mayhew with his right and to get the note with his left hand. Mayhew half turned, let his grip go past, and stuck the note into his pocket.

Byers began to lose the first flush of rage and to get back his equilibrium. His eye made a brief snatch at the crowd, as if to gauge their interest in the scuffle and the chance of anyone's interfering. Then he poised his right fist and let it go solidly from the shoulder. But Mayhew's punch got there a second or so first.

Byers snapped back, came again, more carelessly now, and Mayhew let him have it full force in the chin. Byers' head cracked the glass; a series of little radiating lines shone about him like a halo. His eyes fogged, then cleared slowly. He used the glass as a springboard in his third rush for the detective.

Mayhew pushed him this time, stepped aside, let him come in close, and tripped him. Byers went down headlong, rolled over. For a moment he looked blank, curious, as though something had surprised him out of his anger. One hand fumbled at his coat pocket and came out with a small automatic.

The sound of the exploding bullet coincided with a dull sound of wrenched bone as Mayhew kicked him. For an instant Mayhew stood like a stone, watching the pressing crowd that had made a circle about them, hemming them into a small space against the drugstore. He was waiting for someone to scream, to fall clutching in agony. Byers had rolled upon his face in pain so intense it left no space for sound. His broken wrist trailed under his coat lapel. The gun had spiraled to the building's wall, ricocheted to the middle of the sidewalk.

Mayhew picked up the weapon, broke it and emptied out the remaining bullets and slid bullets and gun into his outer pocket. A uniformed cop was charging the crowd now, blowing his way through with a series of blasts like a broken steam whistle. Collins. Mayhew knew him.

"Break it up, you, break it up. Move on. Hurry up!"

"Collins, give me a hand here, will you?"

Collins withdrew his ire from the unmoving crowd and focused it upon Byers. "Pulled a gun on you, eh? I heard the shot. Anybody hit?"

"Luckily, no." With Collins he got Byers by the shoulders and dragged him to his feet.

An hour later a white and hangdog Byers was ushered into Mayhew's office by an orderly.

"How's the wrist?" Mayhew asked.

Byers' lips barely moved. "It'll be all right. I wasn't going to shoot, you know."

"I couldn't take a chance on that. You had a gun; it proved later to have been loaded. I suppose you have a permit to carry it?"

"I have a permit at home—if it's still good. About two years ago I did some pay-roll deliveries. My company got me the gun and the permit."

"You've carried it since?"

Sunlight, coming in at the side of the shade, made an irregular line down Byers' cheek, bulged suddenly as his jaw tightened. "I used to carry it when I went into that house, the one your Miss Murdock rented. I'd seen Mrs. Ruddick over there. After Alma told me her story I got the idea that Mrs. Ruddick might have the letters hidden there. I took the gun with me several times, unloaded, of course, with the idea that if I could surprise Mrs. Ruddick with the letters I could frighten her into giving them to me."

"And what about today?"

He drew back, and for an instant the bar of sunshine lay across one eye. The dark blue iris stared fiercely at Mayhew. "I didn't know the gun was in my coat. When I fell and rolled over I felt it. I couldn't believe—" He jerked forward. "Some crazy impulse made me pull it out."

"And the fact that it was loaded?"

"I don't understand that at all. So help me—I don't even know where the bullets are at home." The bar of sunlight was on Byers' wrist now, encased in layers of splints and bandages, making a white shine up into Byers' haggard face. "I wouldn't have even tried to fire it, except that you kicked my wrist. There must have been a reflex action of some sort."

Mayhew took a white square of paper out of a desk drawer and spread it for Byers to see.

"Miss Tellingham seems to be little short of psychic," he commented. "Or perhaps she had previous knowledge."

DEAREST RONALD:

I was afraid to talk to you at home this morning. The police are very apt to have your wires tapped, and I do so want to get away, get over this feeling of entrapment that follows me everywhere.

I asked you to meet me, and then at the last moment I saw that that was more dangerous than a telephone conversation. The police mustn't suspect that I am shielding you. You see, my dear, the afternoon that Mrs. Karov died I was in my room, as I said I was, with my back to the window. And across the room was a mirror. Oh, Ronald, why?

Most of all, I am afraid for Claudia. I know you haven't any part in what concerns her. That is strictly a mercenary proposition. Watch over her, won't you?

ALMA

"Well?" Mayhew said when Byers had finished reading.

"It doesn't make sense."

"What did she see you do the afternoon Mrs. Karov was murdered?"

"Nothing. She couldn't have. I didn't kill the woman."

"You haven't been working since all this started, have you?"

"No. The publicity would be too damned unpleasant on my job. I'm sales manager for Cartel and Company—that is, if I've still got a job."

"Where were you this morning when Claudia was injured?"

"I've told you that. I'd gone to the drugstore some blocks away to get a newspaper. We didn't get one this morning."

Mayhew tapped the note lightly. "And this part about Claudia. If Miss Tellingham knows the child is in danger why doesn't she warn the family? Warn Claudia's grandfather and your sister Bernice so that they, too, could keep guard over her?"

"Alma and Bernice never got along. It was mostly a matter of jealousy, quarrels they'd carried over from childhood. My father naturally saw Bernice's side of things. Alma would never be able to go to them about Claudia. They'd tell her it was none of her business."

"What happened this morning is everybody's business," Mayhew said. "The thing that interests me is that Miss Tellingham felt it coming. In a matter of time, of course, it had happened before she wrote this note. But she couldn't have known of it. Even though her mother, who was sleeping at the time it happened, had seen it and told her, she couldn't have said that it had been done deliberately. Only your family know that."

"And, of course, the person who tampered with Claudia's swing."

Mayhew's glance stung. "Providing, of course, the same person doesn't fit in both categories."

Byers' free hand clamped upon the arm of his chair. The sunlight angled across it, gave the effect of a handcuff in yellow. ."You haven't any right to throw suspicion on my family when such obvious motive exists in other directions." The words seemed wrung out of him; they sounded hollow in the space of the little office. "As long as it is money—and it *has to be money*—the simplest solution is that the Tellingham properties are on their way into a control where they will be used to the fullest benefit of the murderer."

"Go on," Mayhew said interestedly.

"Ever since Barbara Tellingham died and left that huge acreage and the other small properties tied up as they were, with a three-member board pulling in three different directions, there has been friction and hatred among the three families. There weren't any murders, however, because the friction kept Alma and me apart, kept out the possibility of our marriage. Only, now"—he flexed his unbandaged arm along the chair as if to relieve an unendurable tension—"now at last we had begun to see each other, to believe in each other again."

"You mean, because of the possibility of your marriage the three-member board was rapidly approaching its end?"

"Yes, If a disposition of the property was to be made it had to be made quickly. The members failed to agree, as they always had. And so they had to be—liquidated." He made a wry face over the word.

Mayhew stood, went to the window, and raised the blind. The room brightened. Below the street was empty and somnolent.

"And you think, then, that one of the remaining members killed Mrs. Ruddick; that a second member will be killed for the same motive?"

Ronald Byers took a long time answering. "If Mrs. Tellingham can get control of her mother-in-law's estate before we marry she can convert it into cash and reinvest as she sees fit. For all practical purposes the money will be hers."

A bell rang in Mayhew's brain. Part of the puzzle had come out into the open. He turned slowly. The other man was staring at the bandages of his broken wrist. If he saw what Mayhew saw he gave no sign.

CHAPTER EIGHTEEN

CLAUDIA'S BREATHING made a ragged sound in the twilight, like a young bird with its head stuffed in among its mother's feathers. She had been sleeping for a long while. The doctor had gone. Bernice and Grandpa were somewhere on the same floor. Miss Rachel felt that probably one or both had their eyes fixed with quiet attentiveness on the door of Claudia's room. They hadn't liked it when the doctor had suggested that Miss Rachel stay. It hadn't been Miss Rachel's idea, either, though she couldn't tell them that. It had been Mayhew's.

Outside, the walls of the old house next door, her house, gave back the twilight with a faint shine of the weathered wood. The rose garden was a wilderness of spidery branches, the earth dark beneath; blue shadow like ink poured about the roots of the hedge that marked the boundary of the Hayes yard. Mr. Hayes was the only thing that moved. His round face bobbed above his shears. The hedge was sturdy stock. It had to be, to endure all the clipping Mr. Hayes gave it.

Miss Rachel leaned her face against the pane. Below were the windows of the cellar where Claudia had seen the little "candly" light carried by her great grandmother on the night of the first murder. The panes were blank now, darkness inside like a curtain against the glass. Withered leaves blew off the vine on the trellis, scattered across the space of earth between the two houses. There was an air of decay, of hopes and dreams gone glimmering, about the scene below.

Miss Rachel sighed, started to turn back into the room.

Mrs. Tellingham came out suddenly upon her rear porch. She was dressed now in a dark frock with touches of white at throat and wrist; her hair was "neat, her feet perfectly shod, but the dishevelment had transferred itself to her walk and posture. No sooner had she gotten outside the door than she fell against it, putting one hand over her mouth. Even at this distance Miss Rachel could see her eyes, enormous in a face like chalk.

Miss Rachel rose out of her chair by the window, made two steps toward the hall before she remembered Claudia. Claudia's face, too, was like chalk, and there was the matter of a broken collarbone to be looked after. Miss Rachel turned again to the window.

Mrs. Tellingham had pushed her way from the door to the edge of the porch, where she stood teetering like a swimmer on the edge of a cold pool. Mr. Hayes had stopped clipping, was staring as if mesmerized at the woman. A gust of wind swept leaves from the dead vine out into the rear yard; Miss Rachel seemed to feel its chill creep up her skin.

Mrs. Tellingham began to run across her yard in an irregular sprint. She crossed the alley, pulled her clothes through the tangle of roses with what must have been considerable expense of fabric, scrambled up Miss Rachel's back steps. The hollow sound of her rapping echoed feebly through the pane.

Miss Rachel went out into the hall. Grandpa sat in his room with the door open. His face was in shadow, the light from behind making dull cotton out of his hair.

"Please," Miss Rachel said quickly. "I'll have to be gone for a minute or so." She watched as he got up slowly. "I can leave Claudia with you, can't I? And she'll be quite safe?"

His eyes were quite unreadable, his gait slow, and when he put a hand on the knob to Claudia's door he gripped it with something like satisfaction. "She'll be quite safe with me. Nothing more can happen to her now." He turned, went in out of sight.

Mass Rachel fought waves of goose flesh all the way to her own back door.

Mrs. Tellingham was in her kitchen with her face under the faucet, gurgling water into her throat. At the sound of Miss Rachel's entry she jerked erect. The water had mottled her make-up, run in rivulets through her hair.

"Oh, it's you. At last." She clung to the sink with both hands. "I've been poisoned. I'm afraid I'm going to die."

"I'll call a doctor," Miss Rachel promised, hurrying past.

Mrs. Tellingham jumped, caught her arm. "No, I didn't quite mean that. Not from the milk, at least. You see, somebody *tried* to poison me." She was shaking as though on the verge of hysteria. "I'll die eventually. Whoever it is will kill me, too, just as they killed Mrs. Ruddick." Miss Rachel watched her carefully, wondering if Mrs. Tellingham were actually as upset as she seemed to be. "You mean you didn't actually take the poison into your system?"

"No, I tasted the milk, and it was queer and I didn't drink it. But being in the house alone and knowing that somebody was after me, tracking me down like an animal . . ." She caught at her lips to stop their quivering. "It's like being in a cage, held there until the hunter gets ready to kill me. I can't stay there alone. Please let me be with you."

Miss Rachel hated to deny such abject pleading. At the same time she felt the pressure of the minutes since she had left Claudia with her grandfather. And there was the milk Mrs. Tellingham had said was poisoned. It should be put away in a safe place until the lieutenant could have it analyzed.

"I'll call Lieutenant Mayhew and see what he says," Miss Rachel told her and pulled the clinging hands off her sleeve. "We'll have to go back to your house to telephone."

Mrs. Tellingham whimpered like a child, but when Miss Rachel started for the door she followed closely. They picked their way back through the garden, dim now with the gradual dying of daylight. Mr. Hayes, at the near end of his hedge, watched, unmoving. On the Tellingham back porch Miss Rachel paused to look back.

There was a light on in Claudia's room. This vexed Miss Rachel. The child needed darkness, quiet. And then as she watched the light went off. Mr. Hayes's clippers began a slow metallic click. Mrs. Hayes had come out upon her rear steps. An odd little tableau followed. Mr. Hayes took his clippers off the hedge and pointed them toward his wife, almost as though he meant them for a weapon. The majesty of Mrs. Hayes's bulk seemed to shrivel in upon itself. Without speaking she went back inside.

The Tellingham house was full of shadow, broken only by the shine of the polished floors where light from the windows crossed them. Miss Rachel felt her way through to the telephone, called the police, asked for Mayhew. But Mayhew wasn't in.

"Meanwhile I'll have a look at the milk," she said to Mrs. Tellingham. On the sink, pushed up under the window, was a glass of milk nearly full. Miss Rachel put it under her nose and sniffed. It was sharp, acrid. She stuck in the tip of her tongue, rolled the drop of liquid tentatively about. Then she took a mouthful. Mrs. Tellingham gasped and drew away. "The milk is sour. Otherwise I can't find much wrong with it."

Mrs. Tellingham tried to control a look of obvious disappointment. "Perhaps it's been changed since I was here."

"I don't see how. You haven't been gone long enough for anyone to have reached this house from the other block by the front door. And we would have seen anyone who came by the back. After all"—her gaze found Mrs. Tellingham's face, both frightened and resentful—"even this murderer isn't invisible."

"Still, I don't want to be alone. I want you with me," Mrs. Tellingham complained.

"Perhaps your daughter will be back this evening," Miss Rachel said while her thoughts flew to Claudia. Claudia, whom she shouldn't have left.

"I don't believe that she will. She's defending *him* in some way." Her nostrils flared. "Why can't he come forward and admit whatever it is he's done? Why must I be left alone because of him?"

"I'll stay for a minute or so," Miss Rachel promised. She tried the telephone again. Still Mayhew was out. "Suppose we go to your room," she suggested, with an idea of getting Mrs. Tellingham to relax. It had worked before; it might again.

The shadows were thick in Mrs. Tellingham's bedroom, but Miss Rachel forbore to turn on any lights. She wanted to get this nerve-racked woman to sleep, or at least at rest, and then to leave her. She pulled down the top coverlet of Mrs. Tellingham's bed.

"Lie down, and I'll stay with you."

"But I'm not sleepy," Mrs. Tellingham complained. "And,

besides, this morning you didn't stay. You slipped off with that policeman."

Miss Rachel wouldn't have described her headlong flight to Claudia as a form of slipping away, but she let it pass.

"You know, I think the lieutenant has an idea that Mother's will is at the bottom of all this," Mrs. Tellingham said, sitting down but making no move to stretch out. "Claudia, you see. By a freak of wording—you can't imagine how stubborn the old lady was—there was a slip-up. If all of us die—the trustees, I mean—a fund has to be set up for the children. Ronald's children as well as Alma's." She picked irritatedly at a tuft on the bedspread. "Isn't that awkward? And unfair too? It's robbing us; that's what it is."

Miss Rachel sat as if frozen. "Do you mean that Claudia is, unwittingly, a cog in that complicated inheritance machine?"

"That's an odd thing to call it." Mrs. Tellingham's gaze was sour. "But, yes, that's about the truth of it." She explained with vindictiveness the workings of her mother-in-law's will.

Miss Rachel got up and walked to the window. Lights were on in the lower floors of the two houses that flanked her own. Mrs. Hayes's big shoulders cast a shadow on the blind in her kitchen, moving slowly with the rhythm of her housekeeping tasks. A dim glow shone from the back of the Byers place—a reflection through from some front room, Miss Rachel thought.

It has to fit together, Miss Rachel thought bitterly. It has to. Somehow, that dark coat, all those extra buttons, the fact that Alma Tellingham thought she had to get away before she betrayed something she didn't want to . . . Her thoughts came to a dead stop. "Wait for me. I'll be close," she said, hurrying for the door.

In Alma Tellingham's room she sat down determinedly in

the lounge chair, let her back touch its cushions, looked fixed-ly into the mirror on the opposite side of the room. The out-of-doors was by now almost completely dark. Her house showed in the mirror as a dim hulk without light or life. On either side were the tiny windows, yellow and glowing, of the other hous-es. Dollhouses couldn't have been smaller and neater, with every detail exact and proportionate.

She was going to wait here, to sense some part of the mon-strous puzzle that had baffled her, itf it took all night. No, it couldn't take all night because of Claudia. She should be with Claudia now. Grandpa had seemed funny and secretive; she re-called his clutch on the doorknob and shivered. Claudia was in such danger. And yet, come to think about it, the things that had happened to the child had been *different*, somehow, from the things that had happened to Mrs. Ruddick and Mrs. Karov. Not murder—just maiming, grieving, spiteful things. Was there more than one infected mind in the triangle of houses on Beecher and Chatham streets?

The curve of the chair against her back was like the press of a comforting hand. After all, she had had practically no sleep last night. Would it hurt so much to relax for a moment?

She never knew just when her eyes went shut.

Minutes later some wave of alarm surged up out of her sub-conscious, and she woke with the sting of unfinished sleep in her eyes. She pulled erect, feeling her body's stiffness. Across the room the mirror twinkled, and the rest was blackness. Nothing had changed in the reflected scene except that the Hayes house was lit from top to bottom.

Miss Rachel sat still and listened, wondering what had awak-ened her. Her heart was beating with a strange, thick rhythm. Had it been a dream? Or perhaps some restlessness on Mrs.

Tellingham's part? She rubbed her eyes, took a deep breath. There was no sound of movement that she could hear.

Her eyes swung back to the mirror, studied it. The Hayes house was dark as pitch, the Byers place lit up as if for a ball. Wait. What had happened in the moment she had looked away? Had all the lights been put out simultaneously in one house, turned on in the other? She moved to the edge of the chair, scarcely breathing.

She had been mistaken in that first glance. She saw now that, drowsy as she had been, she had confused the reflection with reality. In the mirror the houses were reversed. Half asleep, she had forgotten a simple fact, had taken one house for the other.

It was time she was getting back to Claudia.

She pushed herself up and then dropped back abruptly. She had remembered why she had come here. For a long moment she sat quiet, her eyes on the mirror, her figure tense.

"It must be," she whispered to herself. "It's the one thing that explains all of it."

The hallway was dark, and no strip of light shone from under Mrs. Tellingham's door. Miss Rachel went cautiously to the stair well and looked down. Below was not complete darkness. There was a light somewhere, but beyond too many intersecting angles to do much except show the difference between the waxed floor and the paler wall.

Miss Rachel went toward the front of the house. The light proved to be in the living room, where Mrs. Tellingham sat between two floor lamps. She had picked up an unfinished piece of knitting, was working on it in what seemed a very erratic manner. As Miss Rachel watched from the shadows beyond the doorway Mrs. Tellingham removed one of the knitting needles and with it made several short stabs about her. Two or three stabs at some imaginary foe in front of her, one into the pillow at her elbow. She withdrew the needle slowly from the pillow as if savoring the pull of the interior.

Miss Rachel left the house very rapidly by way of the back door.

The Byers place was really lit up to a remarkable degree. Though Miss Rachel could not know it, Mayhew was there with Ronald Byers, trying to force out of him what Alma had seen him do. Miss Rachel had suddenly remembered her cat, long shut up, neglected and hungry. Samantha would be outraged, alone in the unfamiliar house without either breakfast or dinner. There could be little harm, she thought, in making a moment's detour to set out Samantha's supper and to let her free into the garden until bedtime.

She ran up the back steps, hearing the tap of her heels in the hollow space under the stairs. The knob was cool with dew, the interior of the kitchen stuffy with a day's closure.

Miss Rachel snapped the light switch, snapped it again when nothing happened.

"Samantha! Here, kitty, kitty!" She felt about the floor, where Samantha sometimes stood aloof, waiting to see if there was any prospect of food. What had happened to the kitchen light? Was it burned out? Most probably—the globes had been old and dusty when she had first noticed them.

There was a far-off sound of mewing. Miss Rachel went into the narrow passage, then into the cooler space of the front hall. The mewing was definitely not on this floor. It was from upstairs.

How silly of the cat to shut herself in! Miss Rachel went to the light switch by the front door. It clicked under the pressure of her finger, but the dark stayed on.

The lights were *all* gone then! Some defect of wiring, a burned-out fuse, a short where the protective covering had worn through and the wire was raw. Fires could be started that way! Miss Rachel was torn between a desire to investigate the fuse box on the outer wall by the kitchen door and to go ahead and let the cat out. Shut into a single room, Samantha would be raging!

She ran upstairs. The cat was in the empty room where Alma and Ronald had kept their rendezvous. The mewing came out from under the door like a breath of fury, and scratching accompanied it. Miss Rachel said, "Hush. I'm here to let you out," and her hand fixed on the knob and it turned. Easily. Too easily.

Terror pinked her skin, burst in her mind like a fork of lightning.

There was no drawing back in the face of what came out at her, no possible hiding, no step long enough to take her away from the white-hot thing that cleaved her skull. She remembered putting up an arm, crying out as well as she could in the moment left to her. And then a deep soft falling down a vista of rainbows with pain like an arrow just behind her.

With all her strength she thought she said loudly, "This won't help you. Nothing can."

Mind, memory, will, were washing out like the ebb of a tide. "You'll never get away. I know you. *I know who you are at last!*"

CHAPTER NINETEEN

BERNICE BYERS had answered Mayhew's knock. She looked at him frostily, stepped aside. "Won't you come in? Ronald, Claudia's awake and she wants you."

Ronald plodded upstairs. Something had gone out of him—confidence in Alma, Mayhew thought. If Alma actually hadn't seen Ronald from her room at the time of Mrs. Karov's murder, the only other explanation was that she was framing him to protect somebody else. Her mother, for instance. Mayhew made a mental note to look in on Mrs. Tellingham during the course of the evening.

Grandpa met them at the top of the stairs, a grizzled watchdog with a cotton mane. "She wanted the light on," he whispered in Mayhew's direction. "She's been awake for nearly a half-hour."

"Any pain?"

"Not much." Grandpa led the way into Claudia's room. The light was on, but a newspaper had been folded about it to cut off the glare. Claudia lay quiet, watchful. When her father came in she smiled.

"Daddy, you've been gone a long time," she reproached him.

Bernice hadn't followed them upstairs. Her way of showing

pique at his intrusion, Mayhew supposed. He sat down by Claudia's bed and spoke as casually as he was able.

"Do you remember how you happened to be hurt?" he asked.

"Oh, I remember that. Easy. It was my swing. I was going higher and higher"—her eye strayed to the door as if afraid of her aunt's disapproval—"and then the rope broke. It was awful, like a bird without any wings." Her mouth puckered with remembered fear.

"Claudia, I want you to think about this next part very carefully. Don't answer until you've thought hard about it." He took her cool little hand and wrapped it in his big one. "Did you see anybody touch your swing either last night or early this morning?"

She waited obediently until she thought Mayhew's space of time for thought had been filled. "No. I don't think anybody used it."

"Not used it. Touched the ropes, I mean, handled them in any way."

She shook her head, puzzled and somewhat worried over his question. "No. I didn't see anybody."

The swing had been tampered with in the night then. Mayhew rose from the chair and walked to the window. Miss Rachel's house was a dark hulk, the yard at its rear a nest of blackness. Mayhew turned round abruptly.

"If you don't mind, I'd like to look through your place. Give the rooms the once-over." He saw Grandpa stiffen. Ronald, who had taken Mayhew's chair at Claudia's bedside, only shrugged. His face, bent over Claudia's hand, was without visible expression. "It's not aimless prying," Mayhew told them. "I know what I'm looking for."

"Go ahead," Ronald said carelessly.

Grandpa moved to the center of the doorway. "You'll need a search warrant for it, won't you?"

"Let him go, Dad," Ronald said sharply. "If you don't he'll think we have something to hide."

Grandpa moved aside little by little in a crablike movement. In passing Mayhew caught a phrase about the nerve of the damned police. He went out into the hallway, where four doors faced him.

The first room was Ronald's. There was man's attire in the closet, military brushes on the dresser, a rack of ties in the old-fashioned wardrobe. Four pictures of Claudia in various stages of growth decorated the walls. A cabinet photograph of a girl about sixteen faced a fifth picture of Claudia in a hinged double frame. Mayhew looked briefly into the dresser drawers. In the lowest he found a snapshot album, took it out, and leafed it through.

It had been indifferently kept, the pictures put in helter-skelter, without regard to continuity in time or event. Near the front of the book Mayhew found a copy of the picture Mrs. Hayes had shown him, two pages farther on its near duplicate. Seeing the second picture, he was at first inclined to rub his eyes, then inspect the print for signs of double exposure. It showed the group at the beach dressed for leaving, the children standing solemnly in a row with their coats on, the parents behind them loaded with picnic paraphernalia. Mayhew extracted the second picture and left the room.

He stuck his head in where Claudia lay. Only Ronald remained with her. He had his head down on the pillow beside hers, looked half asleep.

"Where's your father?"

He opened his eyes but didn't raise his head. "Downstairs, I suppose."

"Let me know when he comes back upstairs, will you? There's something I want to ask him."

"Sure, I'll tell him."

Mayhew went to the stair-head and listened. There was some sound of movement below, then the gurgle of water running. The old man must have gone down for a drink.

The second bedroom was Bernice's. Mayhew made almost no search here, but he stood for more than a minute before the photograph of Bernice and Ronald as small children which Miss Rachel had noticed on a previous visit.

He hunted for photographs, snapshots, any scrap of likeness, in Grandpa's room and found none. Grandpa ran to notebooks filled with the believe-it-or not type of newspaper feature. Of pictures of his children he had none.

Mayhew put his head in again; Ronald raised his this time. Perhaps some thing in Mayhew's face warned and frightened him. Miss Rachel had said that when Mayhew hit a valid scent his expression lengthened and his patience shortened. "I want you downstairs," he said to Ronald Byers. "I think Claudia will let you go for a minute or so."

Ronald disengaged Claudia's fingers and followed Mayhew to the lower floor. Grandpa came out of the kitchen passage as they reached the foot of the stairs. "Are you through?" he asked.

"Not yet," Mayhew said briefly. "Where is Miss Byers?"

"Bernice is in the living room."

Mayhew strode to the living-room door. Bernice was across the room, at the windows. At the sound of Mayhew's entry she jumped, flung about.

"You frightened me. I'm getting jumpy, I guess." She put her hands on the sill behind her and clung tight, taking a moment to regain control of herself. "Did you wish something of me?"

"Sit down, Miss Byers," Mayhew said gravely. "You gentlemen over there, please."

Ronald fell into the chair Mayhew indicated, but Grandpa stared at the other as though it might bite him. "I'm going to begin by summarizing a little," Mayhew said without showing any interest in Grandpa's behavior. "I think that all of you remember most of the details concerning the murder of Mrs. Ruddick. I suppose, too, that Mr. Byers"—his glance flicked to Ronald—"that Mr. Byers told you about the letters which Mrs. Ruddick had hidden. I am now convinced that those letters were one of the mainsprings of the crime. A certain person took them from Mrs. Ruddick because this person had as strong, if not a stronger, desire to keep Mr. Byers from marrying Miss Tellingham. A more inaccessible hiding place was chosen. Mrs. Ruddick persisted in searching for them. Meanwhile another motive came into being. Mrs. Ruddick was one of three who controlled the Tellingham estate. If two of the trustees could be killed the third would have unlimited control, could buy, sell, trade, or do as he pleased with property worth hundreds of thousands of dollars. Inevitably some of the money could be handled to the benefit of the last trustee. Worthless properties, for example, could be purchased privately by the trustee and resold to the estate at enormous profit. There was literally no limit, save the size of the estate, to what could be done for private gain."

If the three people who faced him were breathing, they gave

no indication of it. There was a stricken immobility to them, an unreal solidity like flesh-colored stone.

"There is no doubt, therefore, that the plans of this murderer included, beside the murders of Mrs. Ruddick and Mrs. Karov, a further murder—that of the second trustee."

Grandpa came alive and began sliding down gradually in the chair Mayhew had chosen for him. He looked as though he wanted to speak and couldn't, as though some paralysis held his tongue.

"Then we have a third phase of the crime, the intention to do harm to Claudia.

I hate this part of it. It's damnable."

He let them sit silent for more than a minute after that. He felt the weight of their fear and uncertainty directed toward him like gigantic tentacles.

"Now as to the murder of Mrs. Karov," he resumed. "We have there a description of the murderer, though it is arrived at strictly by deduction. Alma Tellingham thinks that she saw Ronald Byers go into the house next door at the time Mrs. Karov must have been killed. Obviously this figure must have corresponded in some noticeable respect to that of Mr. Byers."

He took a square of paper from his pocket and held it so that no one but himself could see its inner surface. Grandpa had begun to breathe with the asthmatic constriction of the aged when they are distressed. Bernice was digging her nails into the upholstered chair arms. But Ronald was stonelike, quiet.

"How long has it been, Miss Byers, since you and your brother wore matched clothing?"

She started to rise. Her eyes were on the back of the snapshot in Mayhew's fingers. "Some years," she stammered. "Not since we were very young."

"You had matching coats, didn't you, at about the time you were sixteen and your brother fifteen?" Mayhew's gaze came slowly off the picture to stare at her. "Denying this won't help, Miss Byers. There obviously must be two coats in existence even now. The murderer was seen wearing one by Mrs. Karov, though she couldn't identify it as the duplicate of her own. There was an odd button torn off in Miss Murdock's trellis one night when this same murderer tried to invade her house. It matched the buttons on Mrs. Karov's coat, though none of hers was missing. A clumsy attempt to make it seem that Mrs. Karov had extra buttons for her coat failed because there were *too many*; coat manufacturers add one or two extras, never more. Certainly not four."

Bernice gave up trying to get out of her chair. She stared at Mayhew as though he were at the end of some long perspective. Distance, time, events, must have gone through her mind like a reel of film.

"Wherever you have kept your coat hidden it will be found now. If we have to tear this house down board by board. For obviously a garment worn as that one was will have evidence on it of its purpose." He held the picture out toward her suddenly. "Bloodstains, Miss Byers. Now where is it?"

Alma Tellingham stood just outside the living-room door. Mayhew had heard her come in, had identified her footsteps as those of a young woman, and had surmised who it might be. He turned quickly before she could dodge beyond the triangle of light that fanned out into the hall.

"Just one question for you, Miss Tellingham. Did you see a

figure which you took to be Mr. Byers leave this house and go next door at the time Mrs. Karov must have been murdered?"

She came forward slowly. The light crept from shoe to calf to thigh. She stopped there, the upper part of her body in shadow. "I came back because I am afraid for my mother's safety. There's no use trying to hide or to deny what I saw." Her voice wavered as though the breath behind it had died suddenly. Then it came back strongly: "I saw you, Ronald. I saw you go in to kill Mrs. Karov."

CHAPTER TWENTY

"But you didn't. Not really," said another voice from a position which must have been just inside the front entry. Miss Rachel then tottered out into the light. Her appearance drew a twin shriek of alarm from the women; the men rose, but only Mayhew hurried to her.

She was very bloody, very shaken, and weary. With Mayhew's help she came forward and sat down in the chair he had vacated.

"I'll call a doctor," Mayhew said, rushing off.

She leaned out of the chair to let her voice follow him. "Call all of them, the Hayeses, Mrs. Tellingham. We need them all. Just say it's a routine inquiry." She fell against the chair back and shut her eyes.

Bernice rushed off in the direction of the kitchen and came back with a glass of water. Miss Rachel took it, and over its rim she let her eyes wander about the group that watched her. Alma had come into the room and was standing against the wall behind Ronald's chair. Ronald hadn't sat down again. He was pacing in a jerky stride before the windows. Only Grandpa was seated again. He looked weary, too—wearier than Miss Rachel.

Bernice Byers was fine-drawn, as though she were being pulled, head and foot, in two different directions.

Mayhew came back shortly and stood over her. "What happened to you?"

"The murderer," she said tiredly. "I went looking for the cat—Samantha, you know—and none of the lights in my house would work, and I had to find her in the dark."

Mayhew said something under his breath about the sport of night cat hunting. "She was shut in that upper room. The one you used," she said to Ronald Byers. "It was a trap, of course. I'd no sooner put my hand on the knob than the door flung open and something split my head." She felt tenderly of the region above her forehead, where the white hair lay red and sticky. "Only, you see, it was Samantha saved me, after all. I remember just vaguely an awful cry she made. Furious. She'd been stepped on in the hurry of getting at me. She clawed the thing that had hurt her." She shut her eyes with a sudden feeling of sickness. "I'd look them over for cat scratches. Afterward, of course."

Mayhew drew on the richest part of his vocabulary.

"And so I didn't quite get killed. I must have lain for a while. When I was fully conscious I had already crawled downstairs. I knew somehow you'd be around."

"And what about this person? You saw—you're positive now?"

"I was positive before that. Obviously, that was the motive for my murder. I kept sticking my nose into things that might lead somewhere. I had to be gotten out of the way."

"Who?" demanded Mayhew.

"I'll tell you if I can just keep these bees out of my head." She pressed gently where it ached the most. "You've made too much of Alma's testimony—rather, the testimony she didn't give but thought that she knew. Now, Alma." The girl's chin jerked up; she was deliberately keeping from any look at Ronald. "You were doing what—just before you saw Ronald go in at my back door?"

"I'd been reading recipes for about an hour. My eyes grew tired—not that I didn't still see perfectly well—and I shut them for a moment or so. And when I opened my eyes, there was Ronald. He—"

"Stop there. *From which house did this figure come?*"

"Why, from this house! I recall that part of it perfectly. How could I forget it? It was the house on the—" She made an odd motion with her left hand, but no words followed it. She simply looked at Miss Rachel as though the elderly lady were some very large rabbit from an invisible hat.

The Hayeses came in at that moment, having been admitted by Mayhew, who had hurried to the front door without losing the conversation in the living room, Mrs. Tellingham followed an instant later. She was still, apparently, engrossed in the knitting, for she carried it with her.

Alma looked at the newcomers—especially at one of the newcomers—with horror in her gaze.

"I think you see your mistake," Miss Rachel said quietly. "It's not a difficult one to make when one's attention is dulled or distracted. I made it myself this evening in your room. It was my first real clue to the identity of the murderer."

Mr. Hayes made a brief sound that was meant to be a chuckle. "Why not let the rest of us in on all this? We'd appreciate the joke, probably."

"It's no joke," Mayhew said grimly. "Go on, Miss Murdock."

"Another thing I think you may have failed to consider, Lieutenant, is the fact that Alma's mirror is a good one and her eyesight probably average. Now, mistaking one man for another, providing something about their clothing is identical, isn't hard from where she was sitting with the mirror opposite. But mistaking a woman for a man? It's very improbable. There's the matter of light-colored hose instead of trouser legs, long hair, a different gait—"

Alma said breathlessly, "It was *him—him*."

Mayhew's hard glance went over the group, as much on guard as a man in a cageful of tigers, and suddenly he was looking at Mr. Hayes, and Mr. Hayes no longer looked bland and half amused. Mr. Hayes put a hand toward his handkerchief, let it dart inside and come out holding a gun.

"Mr. Hayes," Miss Rachel said disappointedly, "you have, in theater parlance, spoiled my punch line. I was just about to tell them who you are."

He didn't say anything. His legs tensed; his feet drew up in preparation for rising. And Mayhew's gaze never left him.

"I wanted to point out that Mrs. Karov's coat being around in sight kept Alma unconsciously aware of the fact that it had been Ronald's and that when she saw you creep into my house to kill Mrs. Karov, wearing the coat that you had gotten somehow from Bernice, she thought of course of Ronald."

He bared his teeth in what must have been intended for a grin. Mayhew didn't seem to be moving, but Miss Rachel began to watch the chair under him. One of its legs was slowly angling outward under the stress of his weight. Hayes's grin passed from Mayhew to Miss Rachel. She jerked her eyes off the chair to meet his, and a finger of ice traced its way up her spine.

He was going to kill her, just as he had killed Mrs. Ruddick and Mrs. Karov. "You killed *Mother!*" Mrs. Hayes screamed. "You killed *Mother!*"

"The old battle-ax," he said under his breath. "I had a chance to triple the dough she left us. Oil stack that's due to go up like a kite. To hell with it now. To hell with you."

"Oh, you—you fiend!" she said faintly.

He was half standing, the gun pointing steadily toward Miss Rachel, something about the pose of his body showing that he was almost ready to try for the door.

"You'd better stay here," Mayhew warned. The chair leg angled so that Mayhew seemed on the verge of falling.

"Shut up," Hayes answered. He swung his body slowly, put his back to the door, walked carefully backward until his head was just inside the door-frame. He was getting away. He still meant to kill her, too, Miss Rachel saw: a sort of final revenge for all the trouble he'd been put to by her meddling.

Mayhew's neck thickened with tension as he gathered himself for a leap. Hayes saw it; the gun wavered for a moment. The thing that happened next occurred with fury and dispatch. The cat walked up slowly behind Mr. Hayes and looked at his legs with unfavorable memory. Miss Rachel held her breath. Yes, Mr. Hayes's whole plan was being carefully unbalanced. He was putting his foot back. He was going to step on the cat.

Mr. Hayes's heel caught a few of the hairs on the end of Samantha's tail. The cat rose and pulled angrily. Hayes put the other foot back to save his balance, and it caught a paw. Samantha yowled, struck out with gleaming claws. The gun made a whistling arc as Hayes struck at her. She wrenched away, let the hand have a dig in passing.

Mayhew was going to try to catch him. Miss Rachel felt as

though all the breath she had drawn in seventy years of living was stopped up inside her, bursting. But Hayes, too, had seen. The gun came up with miraculous swiftness and pointed at Mayhew and belched fire and thunder.

The chair had given away an instant before. Mayhew sprawled as the bullet whistled into the wall; then he had gathered himself, and before Hayes could aim and fire again he was on him.

Mrs. Tellingham stood up and screamed and let her knitting drop. Ronald, hampered by his broken wrist, hurried toward the struggling men with some idea of trying to help Mayhew. The gun barked again, muffled, thick. Mayhew disengaged his grip on Hayes and crawled upright. Hayes lay very still, a scarlet stream pouring out of his throat.

Mr. Hayes was dead by his own hand.

Miss Rachel leaned her head into her hands. It was over now, the dreadful waiting and the suspense, the terror at night and the sharp watchfulness by day.

Mrs. Hayes filled the room with sobbing. "I suspected. I was afraid even to stay at night with him. And yet I couldn't be sure. Oh, Mother, poor Mother! And he didn't love Claudia, either, as he should. He thought of her as one of the Byerses, the result of Annie's unhappy life and the cause of her death. And since Mother died he talked constantly of the money that must be set aside for Claudia. He wanted all of it so terribly. . . ." There was somehow a great deal of dignity about the way Mrs. Hayes cried. It was as though a general had broken into tears on the parade ground.

All the Little Meannesses that had been directed at Claudia, then—they were the result of the mother's death and the child's isolation among her father's people.

Bernice, a much more shaken and human Bernice, was kneeling by Mrs. Hayes's chair. "I'm so sorry." It had a tinge of stiffness, but not much. "You can always see Claudia after this. Whenever you wish." A spinsterish hand patted Mrs. Hayes's large work-worn one. "I've been severe, I guess, trying to keep her from being friends with you. But, you see, in a way she was mine, and I haven't had many people to—to love."

It was out, the spinster's secret, the thing that cold questioning couldn't have dragged from her in a thousand years.

Mrs. Tellingham was rolling the knitting into a ball, running the needles through it. "If he'd ever made a move toward me I'd have been ready for him." And Miss Rachel believed her.

Alma and Ronald had stopped together near the windows. There weren't any words between them, just a look of things having run their course and come into a new cycle. The black pane gave back their reflections, moving toward each other like the drift of two boats on slow water. Ronald's wrist was a white-wrapped bundle, his other hand reaching for hers; her face a secretive cameo, not seeing but knowing.

Miss Rachel shut her eyes, and pain descended, an unendurable pressure. "Now *you're* in bed," Claudia said, standing with her eyes big in Miss Rachel's own bedroom.

"I don't seem to get well as quickly as you did." Miss Rachel smiled. Miss Jennifer had come in with a bowl of soup, looking placid and self-satisfied now that she had Rachel safely home.

Mayhew eyed the chair Jennifer had placed for him, tried it carefully, and then let his weight into it. Claudia wriggled up into his lap. "If you're ready to discuss crime," he began, "I think we can clear up an odd or an end today."

"I'm ready," she said briskly.

"Lieutenant." Miss Jennifer rocked some of the soup out into the plate under the bowl in her agitation. "You must promise *never* to let Rachel go off on such a wild-goose chase again." She pinned him with her eyes. "Rachel has no judgment, no sense of fitness. When I think of her staying there in such danger, never so much as telephoning me to let me know if she were still alive—it's too much."

"Go away, Jennifer."

"I did all that I could," Mayhew pointed out. "She's just the way she is, and I can't control her."

"Promise me that next time,'" Miss Jennifer said loudly, her nostrils flaring, "you'll *arrest* her!"

"It's a good idea." And that's as far as he would go.

When Jennifer had flounced away they talked for a while about Miss Rachel's chances for recovery, which were good, and about Mayhew's chances for advancement, which were promising but uncertain. Then Mayhew drifted into the subject of the crime.

"Near the end, when Byers pulled a gun on me, I was almost sure that he was guilty. I've discovered since that Grandpa had filled the gun with bullets and put it into Ronald's pocket as a means of giving his son a little protection in an emergency. It almost *put* him into an emergency. Fortunately for Ronald, he had no intention of pulling the trigger. I realized that too late. My kick was already on its way."

"And what about the coat that Mr. Hayes had found so useful?"

"We found it in his attic. Mrs. Hayes, of course, *had* heard him go out the back and nearly spoiled things right away by saying so. She knew nothing of the coat. Bernice says that it was put out for the charity collection at about the same time Ronald's was. Hayes must have taken it, used it once or twice, and then put it away for so long that everyone forgot about it. It came in very nicely for his work, especially since its duplicate was running around in the open and there was the chance of the two being confused."

"Was there any sign of Mrs. Ruddick's pin having been snagged in it?"

"I think so. There's a torn-out spot near the hem."

"We should have reasoned more from that blue pin than we did, right at the beginning," Miss Rachel pointed out. "Anyone but a member of the Hayes household would have tried to find an opportunity of leaving it in her room, rather than slipping back to the scene of the murder. Not only would it have been safe to do—but, crushed and broken as the pin was, it would have seemed like a valid clue leading toward the Hayeses. He, of course, didn't dare have it in the house for an instant."

"Bernice was the final winner for my money," Mayhew said. "Even when Alma Tellingham said she'd seen Ronald go into your house I figured she'd seen Bernice in a matching coat."

"I reasoned for a while along the same lines," Miss Rachel admitted. "Then it occurred to me that if there had been a duplicate coat it could have been taken just as Mrs. Karov's was, from a charity collection. It wasn't, however, until I woke out of a few minutes' sleep and found that I had confused the houses reflected in the mirror in Alma's room that I really saw the light. I reasoned that instead of protecting Ronald, as she thought she was doing, she was, in fact, protecting Mr. Hayes. Just because of a book of recipes, distracted attention, and tired eyes."

"And a coat out of a Salvation Army box. He couldn't have known about Alma's mirror, of course, but she gave him the most perfect alibi until you made her remember."

Miss Rachel sighed. "Wasn't I foolish to go there in the first place, go through all that danger, and cause Jennifer to have hysterics? They say you could hear her every evening as soon as the night editions came out."

Claudia wriggled down off Mayhew's legs. "Won't you come see us when you're well? I'll miss you awfully. I liked you. Everybody liked you," she added with hasty politeness. Shyly: "I've got a new toad. It lives in the rose bushes."

Miss Rachel's thoughts flickered over a hope of reincarnation among toads. "Have you named him yet?"

Claudia nodded, still shy, but she was bursting with the news. Mayhew knew.

He coughed to keep from laughing out loud.

"I've named her Samantha." She waited for Miss Rachel's smile. "She's a lady toad, I think. And she's awfully brave. Grandpa says she eats pests." Claudia had trouble with the difficult word. She said it again: "Pests."

"With such a name she could do no less," Miss Rachel assured her.

THE END

DISCUSSION QUESTIONS

- What kind of sleuth is Rachel Murdock? Are there any traits that make her particularly effective?

- Were you able to predict any part of the solution to the case?

- After learning the solution, were there any clues you realized you had missed?

- Would the story be different if it were set in the present day? If so, how?

- Did the social context of the time play a role in the narrative? If so, how?

- What role did the geographical setting play in the narrative? Would the story have been different if it were set someplace else?

- If you were one of the main characters, would you have acted differently at any point in the story?

- Did you identify with any of the characters? If so, which?

- Did this story remind you of any other books you've read?

MORE

DOLORES HITCHENS

AVAILABLE FROM

AMERICAN MYSTERY CLASSICS